P9-CBA-180

The Hidden Fortune

7 sisters.
Many mysteries.

#1 The Secret in the Attic
#2 The Hidden Fortune
#3 Stage Fright

. . . and more mysteries to come!

7 Sister Mysteries

The Hidden
Fortune

Ellen Miles

SCHOLASTIC INC.

New York Toronto London Auckland Sydney
Mexico City New Delhi Hong Kong Buenos Aires

If you purchased this book without a cover, you should be aware that this book is stolen property. It was reported as "unsold and destroyed" to the publisher, and neither the author nor the publisher has received any payment for this "stripped book."

No part of this publication may be reproduced in whole or in part, or stored in a retrieval system, or transmitted in any form or by any means, electronic, mechanical, photocopying, recording, or otherwise, without written permission of the publisher. For information regarding permission, write to Permissions Department, Scholastic Inc., 555 Broadway, New York, NY 10012.

ISBN 0-439-35968-6

Copyright © 2001 by Ellen Miles. All rights reserved. Published by Scholastic Inc. SCHOLASTIC and associated logos are trademarks and/or registered trademarks of Scholastic Inc.

12 11 10 9 8 7 6 5 4 3 2 1   1 2 3 4 5 6/0

Printed in the U.S.A.   40

First Scholastic printing, November 2001

For my mother, Betty Miles,
with much love

Prologue

Katherine got a letter. So did Viola and Helena. And Juliet and I each got one, too.

There are seven of us Parker sisters, but only five of us still live at home. Both Miranda, my oldest sister (she's twenty-one), and Olivia, who's nineteen, were too old to get letters. But Katherine's fourteen, I'm thirteen, Juliet's eleven, and the twins, Viola and Helena, are nine. So we were all within the age range.

"The age range for *what*?" you're probably asking.

The search for the hidden fortune, that's what!

Sit tight, and I'll explain the whole thing. It all began one dreary day in November. . . .

Chapter One

That day had not gotten off to a good start. I woke to the sound of rain clattering against the windows. Very onomatopoeic[1], but not especially pleasant.

"Ugh," Juliet, my eleven-year-old sister and roommate, groaned, from her bed on the other side of our room. She put her pillow over her head. "Mbl *hdlh* nbvduldh."

"What?" I asked. "You know I can't hear you when you're talking through your pillow."

"I *hate* November," Juliet repeated, holding her pillow away from her face for one second. Then she lay back again.

I'm not wild about it, either. November in Vermont always seems to be chilly, gray, and boring. Autumn is over; all the beautiful red and yellow leaves are nothing but a memory. Winter is yet to come. There's no snow, no sun, nothing to do but stare out at the bare trees. Some Vermonters call

---

[1]onomatopoeic: a word that sounds like what it means. *Clatter, buzz, clank, pitter-patter.* (I'm a word lover, and I collect interesting words. I'll be sharing my collection along the way. If you like words, too, great. If you don't care, you can just skip these footnotes!)

this "stick season," because that's all you see everywhere: brown and gray sticks against a gray sky and brown hills.

Lovely.

"Can't I just stay in bed and hide in my room all day?" Juliet asked. She'd tossed the pillow aside by then.

"*Our* room," I said. It bugs me that lately Juliet is always referring to this room as hers. We've been sharing it for a while now.

"Whatever." Juliet yawned. "Anyway, can't I?"

"Take a guess," I said. "How would Poppy answer that question?"

Juliet didn't need to think too long to figure that out. Our dad is not the type to accept "I hate November" as an excuse to stay home from school. She heaved herself out of bed and headed for the door, trailing her blanket behind her.

Another wonderful November day had begun.

Cut to three hours later, at school. I was in social studies, staring out the window at the gloomy gray sky, when the classroom loudspeaker started sputtering. I swear, the sound system at U-28 (that's my school) must be left over from the fifties. "Attention," said a voice through the static. I thought I recognized it as Mrs. Deaver's. She's the school secretary. "Would Ophelia Parker please report to the office? Ophelia Parker to the office, please."

My friend Zoe turned around to look at me. "What'd you do?" she whispered. "Rob a bank? Cheat on your health quiz? Run for it! Don't let them catch you!"

I just looked at Zoe and shook my head. Then I gathered my books together and stood up.

"Go ahead," said Mr. Fields, my teacher. "Zoe can give you the homework later."

I walked out of the room. It was a little embarrassing to know that everyone was watching and wondering. Social studies has been pretty boring lately, so an announcement like that provides big drama, relatively speaking.

I wasn't nervous, exactly. I didn't think I'd done anything wrong. But I was definitely curious. Last time I got called out of class it was because Helena had broken her wrist playing dodgeball at recess and nobody at her school could locate my parents or any of my older sisters.

"Ophelia," said Mrs. Deaver when I got to the office. "There you are." She looked at me over her half-glasses. "Your dad wants you to call home. No big emergency, he said. But he needs to talk to you." She pushed the phone on her desk toward me. "Go ahead. You can call from right here."

I dialed, and Poppy picked up after just one ring. "Oh, good," he said once he heard my voice. "Listen, sweetie, here's the thing. I just got a call.

Plane crash in Pennsylvania. I have to leave in about an hour."

My dad's an investigator for the FAA, the Federal Aviation Administration. This call meant he'd be gone for at least a couple of weeks. "Will you be home for Thanksgiving?" I asked. I hate it when Poppy's not home for holidays.

He paused. "I don't know," he said. "I haven't even thought about that. Right now, I'm concerned about today. Your mom's working late and so is Miranda. Olivia has a class."

Mom and Miranda both work for the Cloverdale police, Mom as a dispatcher and Miranda as an officer and detective-in-training. Olivia lives in Burlington, where she's studying photography.

". . . And Katherine —"

"Has plans," I finished. Katherine, who's a mere eleven months older than me, *always* has plans. And her plans usually involve a boy. I haven't even had one official date yet in my life; Katherine is the most popular girl in eighth grade. I'm not the most *anything* in seventh grade. Well, maybe I'm the girl with the frizziest hair. Or the biggest vocabulary.

"So you need me to be home when the twins and Juliet get home from school," I continued. "I'll make sure Bob gets walked, and make dinner."

Bob's our dog, in case you're wondering. We also have two cats, Jenny and Charles. The twins and Juliet all go to the elementary school, which goes up to sixth grade. The twins are in fourth, and Juliet's in sixth. I'm smack in the middle of my family. And everything else, too. I'm average height; I have average looks. Okay, maybe I have slightly above-average intelligence. I sometimes wish I were one of those standout people: great athlete, major brain, fabulous beauty. But I'm not. I'm just good old Ophelia, the one my parents depend on in times like this.

"That's my girl," Poppy said. "Could you?"

"Sure," I said. Zoe and our friend Emma and I had planned to stay after school to work on our science fair project, but I knew they'd understand. They're used to the fact that I have family responsibilities.

So that's how I ended up making dinner while Juliet read the letter out loud. If I wanted to get dinner on the table at a reasonable hour, I couldn't stop to read.

The letters, all in identical crisp white envelopes with our names and addresses neatly typed, had been waiting in our mailbox when we arrived home from school.

Helena and Viola grabbed theirs and ran off to the living room to lie on the couch and read them.

Juliet put Katherine's aside for when she came home, and handed me mine while I rustled around in the kitchen, opening and shutting cabinets and the fridge as I assembled the ingredients for the lasagna I was going to make.

One glance was enough to tell me that the letters inside the envelope were the same, down to the return address, so I gave it back and asked her to read to me while I worked.

"James Grover?" I asked, before she began. "Isn't that — *wasn't* that Grandpa Grover's real name?" The name on the envelope seemed familiar.

Juliet drew in a breath. "It was!" she said. "I remember reading his obituary just a couple of weeks ago!"

"And now we're getting a letter from him?" I asked, staring at it. "Like, from beyond the grave? That's weird."

Juliet looked at her letter. "Sad, too," she said.

"Yeah," I said. "Grandpa Grover. He was the best crossing guard. I saw him every single day from kindergarten to sixth grade, and he always smiled and waved and asked how I was. He knew everybody's name, too." I felt kind of bad that I'd forgotten all about Grandpa Grover. He was this sweet old man with white hair and a big white handlebar mustache. You wouldn't think a little town like Cloverdale has enough traffic to make a crossing guard necessary, but there happens to be one pretty busy street right by the school. And Grandpa Grover was always there, making sure we were safe.

"He once told me I looked just like his little sister, back when she was young," Juliet remembered. "He always called me 'Sis' after that. But I haven't seen him since last spring. He must have been sick for a while."

"Poor Grandpa Grover." I leaned against the counter, holding the mozzarella cheese I'd just gotten out of the fridge.

"Not so poor," Juliet corrected me. She'd been reading ahead in the letter.

"What do you mean?"

"It turns out that he had quite a fortune when he died, according to this." She pointed to the page. "The crossing guard job was just something he did for fun, after he retired."

"What did he do before he retired?" I asked. This was all news to me.

"He was the president of a huge company that made parts for airplanes," Juliet told me, after checking the letter.

"Whoa!" Dear old Grandpa Grover wasn't quite what he had appeared to be.

"'I grew up in Cloverdale,'" Juliet read from the

letter, "'and loved the town dearly, which is why I came back here when I retired. I never married or had children, but I always loved children. That's why I was a crossing guard. And that's why I created a treasure hunt for the children of Cloverdale. A treasure hunt to find my fortune.'"

"Treasure hunt?" I was in the middle of grating the mozzarella while the lasagna noodles boiled and the tomato sauce simmered. I reached over to turn on the oven so it would be nice and hot when I put the lasagna in. Then I stopped what I was doing to read over Juliet's shoulder. As we read, we both got more and more excited. Grandpa Grover had sent letters to just about every kid in Cloverdale, from ages eight through eighteen. He stated the rules: Younger and older siblings could help, but official teams would have to be made up of four kids between those ages. The letter didn't say exactly what the hidden fortune was, but Grandpa Grover hinted that it was very, very valuable. The first clue would be printed on page eight, section one, of the next day's newspaper, and each clue after that would be revealed along the way. In other words, you wouldn't be able to get the second clue without solving the first one. Each clue would involve not only a hunt for a particular place or thing, but a task that had to be done before the clue was considered solved. There would be four clues in all. The team that solved the final clue first would discover the treasure.

"That's us," Juliet said.

"What's us?" I asked.

"The winning team. How about it? Want to team up? You're smart, and I never give up. We'll be a great combination."

I was a little surprised. Juliet has been sort of pushing me away lately. "Okay," I said. "Sure." Just then the timer dinged, telling me that the lasagna noodles were ready.

Suddenly, November was looking a lot more interesting.

All my other sisters agreed. Katherine breezed in just as I was putting the lasagna on the table, announcing that she intended to win the treasure hunt. She'd already heard about it from her friend Amy, who'd gotten a letter. Helena and Viola had already decided to team up with a couple of friends from school. Olivia called while we were eating dessert, and I told her all about the hunt for Grandpa Grover's fortune. When Miranda stopped by after work to mooch some lasagna, we speculated[2] about what the treasure might be. And we all talked about what it would be like to be

[2]speculate: consider, think about, and try to predict

rich: Katherine said she'd never wear hand-me-downs again, and Juliet figured she'd buy herself a grand piano to replace the electronic keyboard she practices on.

After dinner, I headed into the study to check my e-mail. There was a note from Poppy, thanking me for being "so reliable." He and I always e-mail a lot when he's away. I wrote him back a quick note:

To: DParker
From: WrrdGrrl
Subject: Big Fun
Did you hear about the hidden fortune? Probably not. I guess it wouldn't have made the national news. You won't believe it. A townwide hunt for a mysterious fortune. Wouldn't you love to have a billionaire in the family? We'll get the first clue tomorrow. More then — O.

Chapter Two

The phone started ringing as soon as I got off the computer. The first call was for me.

"So? Are we a team?" It was Zoe, skipping right to the chase, as usual. Zoe doesn't waste words. She doesn't have time. She's always playing or practicing field hockey, soccer, basketball — she's awesome at just about every sport known to man (oops! I mean woman). Zoe's a mesomorph[3] who towers over me — and over most of the boys in seventh and even in eighth grade. She has a big personality to match.

"Sure!" I said. "I mean, I have to check with Juliet. We already decided to team up."

"How about you, me, Emma, and Juliet? With a team like that, we can't miss."

It sounded good to me. I checked with Juliet, and she agreed. She likes my friends, especially Emma. Emma's quiet, but not shy. She's small, but not meek.

For example, one time some kids were calling her "Little Emma" for a while because there's an-

[3]mesomorph: a big-boned, muscular person

other Emma, Emma Woodard, who's more Zoe's size. Emma didn't like it, and she let people know. Now she's just Emma, and Emma Woodard is Emma Woodard.

Emma doesn't feel the need to talk all the time. She's a good listener and a careful observer. Combine that with Zoe's extreme energy, and we were set.

(Note that, once again, I am in the middle. My two friends both consider me their best friend, which puts me in the middle. I'm also in the middle in terms of height. And their incredible talents sometimes make me feel more average than ever. Zoe's probably going to be a starter on the JV basketball team this year, which is unheard of for a seventh-grader. And Emma will probably get Highest Honors every marking period during her career at U-28.)

Anyway, forgive the excursus[4]. I called Emma and we agreed to get together the next day to work on the first clue. She promised to call Zoe and tell her the plan. As soon as I hung up, the phone rang. It was Matthew Kemp calling for Katherine.

He was the first of about fifteen boys to call, hoping for a spot on Katherine's team. It was truly

[4]excursus: a detour from the main subject

amazing to watch her handle all that attention. She's so smooth! No doubt she had already decided exactly which boys she wanted on her team, but she made every boy who called feel like he had a chance. "How sweet, Matthew," she said, for example. "Let me think about it. Can I let you know tomorrow?"

Matthew didn't have a chance. He's had a major crush on Katherine for years, but he's not her type. Still, Katherine's not one to cross anyone off her list who might come in handy later.

Michael Stebbins didn't make the cut, either. Neither did Andy Shapiro, Zoe's older brother, or Anthony Marks. By the time we went to bed, Katherine had narrowed it down to Ryan Cooper and Pete Pelkey. I knew she was saving the fourth spot for Billy Smallwood, the cutest boy in the eighth grade.

When I woke up the next morning, Juliet's bed was already made. I rolled over to check the clock. It was only seven-thirty! Juliet *always* sleeps late on Saturdays. Then I remembered. This was the day we were supposed to get the first clue! I jumped out of bed, threw on my red terry bathrobe (so old that it's more pink than red now, but *so* comfy), and ran downstairs.

"Is it here yet?" I asked Juliet when I found her in the kitchen. She and Viola were having breakfast.

"The paper? Nope." She went back to reading the Cheerios box. Viola was still finishing the crossword from the day before.

"Are you sure?" I asked. The paper usually comes first thing on Saturdays.

"I just checked," she said. "But you can look again."

I went to the front door and got there just as Katherine did. *"You're* up?" I asked, amazed. Katherine rarely shows her face before eleven on Saturdays.

She shrugged. "I thought I'd go for a run," she said. "Just out to Buttercup Road and back. You know, get some exercise."

Sure enough, she was dressed in a sweatshirt, tights, and running shoes. Her hair was pulled back in a perfect ponytail. There were no pillow creases in her face. She doesn't have an athletic bone in her body, but she looked like a Nike ad. How does she do it?

"You *hate* running," I pointed out.

She shrugged.

"I know what you're up to," I blurted out as realization finally broke into my foggy brain.

16

"You're going to ambush the paper boy so you can be the first to see the clue."

"Clue?" Katherine asked, all innocent. Like she'd forgotten all about the treasure hunt.

"You're too late, anyway!" Viola called from the kitchen. "Helena's already out there."

Katherine made a face. "I should have guessed," she said. "Oh, well." Yawning, she kicked off the running shoes and padded into the kitchen for breakfast.

Helena's always up at the crack of dawn. The rest of us have grown used to seeing her glowing face and hearing her peppy chatter while we droop over our cereal bowls.

Helena burst in while I was checking the fridge for strawberry yogurt. It's everybody's favorite flavor, so it goes fast, but I'd tucked a container behind the milk last night. "Forget it!" she exclaimed, throwing the newspaper onto the kitchen table. "If they call *that* a clue . . ." She snorted and plopped herself down into a chair.

Juliet and Katherine grabbed the newspaper at the same time, but Juliet managed to pull it away. I gave up on my yogurt search and looked over her shoulder at the paper she was clutching. The clue, in the form of a short poem, was featured in a small box on page eight. Juliet and I read silently.

Where nightshade joins the meadow rue,
A task will earn the second clue.
A Blossom once, a Bird today,
My crown of jet now gone to gray,
Dear ones gone now from my side,
Their children's children run and hide.
Roosevelt's words on fear are true,
You'll know that when you solve this clue.

"What?" Juliet stared at the words. "What is this supposed to mean?"

I shook my head. I was as confused as she was.

"Let me see it," demanded Katherine. You could tell she thought we were just being dense.

Juliet handed over the paper. "Be my guest," she said, folding her arms across her chest. "There's no way we can figure that out."

"Wait a second. Who just told me she never gives up?" I gave Juliet a little smack on the shoulder.

"Must have been somebody else," Juliet said, smiling. "No, it was me. And of course I'm not giving up. But this isn't going to be as easy as I thought."

Katherine looked up from the clue. "This isn't exactly Shakespeare," she said, frowning. "In fact, it could have probably been written by Shakespeare's dog."

Trust Katherine to critique the writing style. I mean, she was probably right. She knows a lot more about poetry than I do, and even writes some pretty good poems herself. But, really, was that the point? How good the rhymes were?

The phone rang. It was Zoe. "Did you see it?" she asked. "Can you believe it? Is that really the whole clue? This fortune better be *huge* if all the clues are going to be this hard."

"I know," I said. "But we'll figure it out. Meet us at the library at —" I glanced at Juliet. "Ten?" Juliet nodded. "Ten," I repeated to Zoe. "Call Emma, okay?"

The phone rang again. It was Helena's friend Megan. While they were talking about the clue, Mom finally came downstairs. "What's going on?" she asked, tightening her bathrobe belt as she scuffed along in her slippers. Her hair was sticking up in back, and her eyes were puffy. Mom's always a little slow to get started after she works the late shift.

Viola filled her in on the news about the treasure hunt. Then I showed her the first clue.

She read it to herself. "Hmm," she said. "Good luck, everybody." She poured herself a cup of yesterday's coffee, zapped it in the microwave, and headed back upstairs.

The phone rang again, and Katherine grabbed it. "Billy!" she said. "Well, I don't know. I think my team is set already." She paused, as if thinking. "Wait a second — that's right, we *do* need a fourth person, now that I think of it."

Juliet and I rolled our eyes at each other. Once again Katherine had gotten her way. Billy must have read the clue and decided that being on Katherine's team was his only chance. He may not be "the sharpest tack in the box," as Poppy likes to say, but he knows Katherine has brains as well as beauty.

So. The teams were set, we had the first clue, and the race was on. There was only one problem: We had no idea where the starting line was!

By ten-thirty, my team was already falling apart. We met at the library, as planned. But the only thing we agreed on was that we were clueless about the clue.

We were in the reference area, where I always think you should be able to find the answer to any question. Or if you can't, Ms. Rosoff, the librarian, usually can. Only we couldn't ask her for help on this one. It would be against the rules.

Our library's reference section is excellent. This

library, which is over on First Street near the elementary school, was only built a few years ago. They moved all the books over from the tiny old library and upgraded the reference collection. Unfortunately, after that they kind of ran out of money, so there aren't too many kids' books yet in the beautiful new children's room.

"It makes no sense at all," Zoe complained, looking at the scrap of paper she'd clipped from the newspaper.

"I think it will once we start figuring things out," Emma said quietly.

"But how?" Juliet asked.

"We just have to start," I said. "First of all, this line makes it sound as if this person is somebody kids are afraid of. 'Their children's children run and hide.'"

Everybody nodded. Except Emma.

"It might not be a person," she said.

"What do you mean?" I asked. "Of course it's a person."

"It might be a thing," Emma said. "Riddles sometimes sound like they're about people, but they're not. You know, like Little Nancy Etticoat."

We all stared at her. "Who?" Juliet asked finally.

"Little Nancy Etticoat," Emma repeated. Then she stood up and recited the whole poem for us. "Little Nancy Etticoat, in a white petticoat and a red nose. The longer she stands, the shorter she grows." Finished, Emma took a little mock bow and sat down again.

Emma was losing it. I had no idea what she was talking about.

"It's a candle!" she said. "My mom used to tell me that riddle. Didn't you ever hear it?"

None of us had, so she explained it. Turns out, the poem isn't about a girl. It's about a white candle with a red flame. And the longer a burning candle stands, the shorter it gets.

"Wow," said Zoe. "Now I get it. So you're saying that our riddle could be about something other than a person. Like, it could even be about a place. A scary place." She jumped up and started pacing. "What about the abandoned slate quarry?" she said. "That place is pretty creepy. And there are some scary stories about it. And — and the slate is gray!"

"Hold on, hold on," I said. "Let's not get into wild conjecture."

"Wild *what*?" asked Zoe.

"Conjecture," I mumbled. "Guessing." Maybe this wasn't the best time to show off my vocabulary.

"Got a better idea?" Juliet asked drily.

"As a matter of fact, I do," I said. "We're in a library, right? Well, I think we should look a few things up. Like nightshade, for example. 'Where nightshade meets the meadow rue.' Let's find out more about that. It's a plant, isn't it? It sounds like it's poisonous. Maybe that means something. Meadow rue must be a plant, too. And what does 'jet' mean here, where it says, 'my crown of jet now gone to gray'? It's probably not like the airplane kind of jet. And what about this Roosevelt thing? His words on fear? We have to look that up, too."

We got to work. Emma grabbed one of the big dictionaries from its stand. Zoe went to find a book on plants. I tracked down a book of quotations. Juliet just sat there, staring at the poem. She'd taken out a notebook and a pen, and she was ready to write.

"Okay," I said after I'd spent a few minutes looking things up in the index of my book. "There are a bunch of Roosevelt quotes in here, both Franklin and Theodore. But I only see one that makes sense for this clue. It's when Franklin Roosevelt said that 'the only thing we have to fear is fear itself.' I think what the clue is saying is that we have to face our fears and go to this place, or this person, or whatever."

"Good, good," said Juliet, writing it down.

"Nightshade," Zoe read out loud from her wildflower book, "is a vine, a climbing plant. Otherwise known as bittersweet nightshade. There's also something called *deadly* nightshade." She held up a picture. "It's pretty, isn't it? Purple and yellow flowers. But you're right, Ophelia. It *is* poisonous. And meadow rue, as far as I can tell, is a flowering plant in the buttercup family."

Juliet was scribbling away. "Vine," she said. "Purple and yellow. Bittersweet. Poisonous. Rue equals flowering buttercup."

"Okay, and I found 'jet,'" said Emma. "It's a kind of coal. Very black. So the word also means black." She leaned over to watch as Juliet took notes.

So did Katherine, who had just come into the library followed by three boys. "Hey!" said Juliet, covering up her paper. "Do your own research."

Katherine just laughed and arranged herself at a table at the other end of the room. Her myrmidons[5] sat down, too, waiting for orders.

"Okay," said Juliet, ignoring them. She read back from her notes. "So we've got a vine, a poisonous one, meeting another plant. If we go to the place where they meet, our bad dreams will go away. A gray crown was once black — or maybe it was coal — and the only thing we have to fear is fear itself."

---

[5]myrmidons: devoted followers, named after Greek warriors

"Right," I said. "Now it's all clear. Clear as mud."

"What about this blossom part?" asked Emma. "What could that mean?"

"I don't know," I said. "I'm still working on the crown. What if it's somebody's hair? Like, they used to have black hair, and now it's gray? So it's an old person."

"*If* it's a person," Emma said under her breath. "It could be a gray house."

We worked all morning, but by the time the library closed we weren't any closer to solving the first clue. I saw a lot of other kids come and go, but nobody else seemed to be finding the answers, either. Maybe the hidden fortune was going to stay hidden forever.

Chapter Three

"So then, as I was checking my nose for visible boogers, I tripped over my crush and fell, tearing my pants so my Scooby-Doo underwear showed!" Zoe was laughing so hard she was snorting a little.

"Good, good!" cried Emma. "Only we should add something about how the whole school was watching —"

"Because it was halftime at the football game!" I said. "Or, no! It was at the prom!"

"Nobody wears pants to the prom," Zoe pointed out.

"Okay, so she tore her formal gown!" My stomach hurt from laughing so much. "No, she tripped over her gown and knocked her crush into the punch bowl!"

Okay, so maybe you had to be there. Trust me, it was pretty hilarious. Emma, Zoe, and I were over at Zoe's house for a sleepover that Saturday night. We had already eaten (macaroni and cheese from a box, plus brownies we'd baked, with Ben and Jerry's cookie dough flavor on top — no wonder my stomach hurt!), and we'd given up on talking about the clue after I pointed out that it wasn't really fair without Juliet there. I think we were happy for the excuse: The clue was so frustrating that we just wanted to forget about it for a while. Instead, we were up in Zoe's room painting our toenails and reading some of her old teen magazines, taking the quizzes and checking our horoscopes. That's when we started talking about those "My Most Embarrassing Moments" stories.

Zoe always insists that the stories are made up. "It's like there's a formula for them. You know, they always talk about the same things: their crush, some kind of embarrassing body thing, their underwear showing."

"And they're always falling or tripping or something," Emma added. "You're right. It's like they all follow the same rules."

"We should write our own," I said. "I mean, my most embarrassing moments aren't nearly as interesting as most of these. Like" — I thought for a second — "forgetting my lines when I was the teapot in our preschool play."

"I remember that!" Emma said. She and I have been in the same class since we were abecedarians[6] back in preschool. We both went to Tinky's, out near the fire station. Tinky had a llama, of all

---

[6]abecedarian: someone who is learning the alphabet

27

things, for a pet. "You started to cry. And your dad had to come up on stage and give you a hug before you would stop."

"Get out of here!" Zoe said. "Really? I would have died." Zoe moved here from Pennsylvania in fifth grade. So she missed that charming little episode in my life.

I blushed. "Okay, so maybe it was a little embarrassing. What about you guys?"

Zoe grinned. "Once I threw up on this guy's shoes."

"Eww!" Emma and I shrieked. "What guy?" I asked. "Was he your *crush*?" That set us off again. When Zoe caught her breath, she explained.

"No way!" she said. "He was this skinny old guy who was running the ride I went on at the World's Fair."

"You mean this just happened this year?" I asked. We'd all gone to the Tunbridge World's Fair in September. With a name like that, you might think the fair is a really big deal, but it's actually just like any other state fair, with rides and games and booths selling fried dough and other yummy stuff. The World's Fair is a Vermont institution. You *have* to go, every September. You go on all the rides, check out the cows and chickens and giant pumpkins that the 4-H kids bring, and eat greasy food until you can practically *feel* the zits popping out on your face.

Zoe nodded. "It was the day I went with my cousins," she said. "We all went on that ride, the one where you stand there strapped into your own little cage and it spins around until you're totally upside down."

I remembered that ride. I felt like hurling after I went on it. If I'd had one more order of onion rings, I probably would have.

"So what did the guy *do*?" asked Emma.

Zoe shrugged. "Nothing, really. Just shook his head like he was used to it. Which he probably is." She dabbed her big toe with sparkly purple polish. "So? What about you, Emma?"

"What *about* me?" she asked.

"You know. What's your most embarrassing moment?" Zoe was concentrating on her toes, so she didn't see the look Emma and I exchanged. But she noticed the silence. "What?" she asked, looking up at us.

Emma gave me this pleading gaze, like, *Please, don't tell.* Zoe saw it. She put down the little blue bottle. "Okay, give it up. What happened? And when?"

"Second grade," Emma confessed. She was already blushing. "I was scared of our teacher, Mrs. MacGregor."

"She was the *meanest*," I interrupted to tell Zoe. "You wouldn't believe the stuff she did. She once made Peter Brown stand in the corner for two hours, just for forgetting his homework."

"So?" Zoe urged Emma on.

"So I brought my teddy — his name was Dinky — to school, like as a security blanket?" Emma said. "I hid him in my backpack. But she caught me reaching in to check on him one time and made me take him out and introduce him to the whole class. It was so embarrassing. I felt like a big baby."

Zoe stared at her. "That's awful," she said.

"I know," Emma said. "Everybody's pretty much forgotten by now, but once in a while somebody still calls me 'Dinky's Mom.'"

She looked so miserable I tried to hold in my giggles. But when I met Zoe's eyes, we both cracked up. "You guys!" said Emma. But then she started laughing, too. What else can you do?

Anyway, we spent a while that night writing the most outrageous Embarrassing Moments we could think of. (I can't even repeat most of them here. . . .) We laughed so hard and so loud that Zoe's brother, Andy, finally came into her room to tell us to quiet down. Of course, *that* was embarrassing, mostly because he saw Emma and me in our pj's. The next morning, I was laughing to myself as I walked home. I could hardly wait to tell Juliet.

I headed up to our room to find her and change clothes. The door was closed, but I opened it and walked in — and had the surprise of my life.

Chapter Four

"Hey!" I said. "What's going on?"

I've always loved our room. It's a big rectangle, with two windows along one side. The wallpaper's yellow, with these weird little squiggly white flowers. Each of our desks is beneath a window, looking out, and our beds are opposite our desks, headboards against the wall. There are white curtains at the windows, and my quilt is mostly blue while Juliet's is mostly green. There's an oval braided rug in blue, green, and purple between our beds. We each have an inflatable chair, mine with blue daisies on it and Juliet's with green. We each have a bureau next to our beds, and a bookshelf along the other wall. We share the big closet on Juliet's side, and we both stick up posters and ticket stubs and pictures of our friends on a bulletin board between our beds.

When I wake up in the morning, the first thing I always do is look over at Juliet's bed. If she's awake, she'll look back at me and smile — or groan if the alarm has gone off before she's ready. If she isn't awake, there's something comforting about seeing the big lump her body makes under her blankets.

Juliet and I have always gotten along, as roommates and as sisters. Living with her is the complete opposite of living with Katherine, which I did until fourth grade. Katherine and I fought all the time, about anything and everything. Eventually Mom and Poppy started to worry that one of us might defenestrate[7] the other, and they separated us. Katherine doubled up with Olivia until Olivia moved out, and now Katherine has that room mostly to herself, except when Miranda or Olivia come to visit and end up staying over.

Juliet and I never fight. Well, hardly ever. We're used to each other's ways. I know she snores for a while when she first falls asleep, but then she always stops. And she's used to the fact that I sometimes sleep with my pillow over my head; if I don't hear the alarm she comes over, picks up the pillow, and whispers into my ear until I wake up.

Juliet doesn't mind when I practice the flute, and I don't mind when she plays her keyboard. We both like to read in bed before we go to sleep. If either of us wants the room to herself for a while,

[7]defenestrate: to throw out a window

we just say so. And if we decide to change things around, we always do it together — like when we traded desks a while ago.

All of this is to explain why I was so shocked when I walked in that morning to see that everything was completely — and I mean *completely* — different.

My bed was right up near the door, and Juliet's was way on the other side of the room, with the back of its headboard facing my side. She'd moved our bookshelves and bureaus to form a low wall down the center of the room, mine facing my bed and Juliet's facing hers. The bulletin board was now on the wall on my side, but everything on it was mine. Juliet had taken all her things off it. And our desks, instead of being next to each other under the windows, were facing in opposite directions.

"What's going on?" I said as soon as I'd gotten over being totally speechless.

Juliet stood up from behind her bookcase, where she must have been arranging her books. "Oh, hi, Ophelia," she said. "What do you think?" She gestured around at the room.

"What do I *think*?" I asked, folding my arms. "I *think* you should have asked me, or at least talked to me, before you did anything so drastic."

"Sorry," she said, ducking back down.

"Sorry?" I asked. "Wait a second, Juliet. What's this all about? It's like you're turning your back on me, trying to pretend I'm not in the same room as you." Suddenly, I felt really hurt. I thought Juliet liked being my roommate as much as I liked being hers, but obviously I was wrong. By moving all that furniture around, she'd made her point. She was hiding from me, cutting me off.

She stood up again and faced me, all serious. "I just — don't laugh, okay?"

I was far from laughing. "What?"

"I need my personal space," she finished.

"Oh, right," I said. *Personal space* is kind of a Parker family joke. Why? Because there just isn't any, when so many people are sharing a house meant for a *regular*-sized family.

"No, really," said Juliet, hugging a book to her chest.

"So you have to make me feel like I'm totally not wanted?" I asked.

"I didn't mean to —"

"Well, you did." I flopped down on my bed. Lying there, I felt like I was behind a big barricade. I couldn't even see Juliet's bed. Everything was different. How was I supposed to feel, when my own sister didn't want to share a room with me? What was I supposed to do? For a second, I wondered if I should move back in with Katherine. Just for a second. Then I caught myself. We already knew how well *that* would work out.

"I thought we were teammates," I mumbled, hugging Doogey, the stuffed dachshund I've had on my bed since I was three.

"We are," Juliet answered from behind her bookcase.

"I wouldn't let Emma and Zoe discuss the clue last night because you weren't there," I remembered. "I stuck up for you."

"Thanks," she said.

"Now I wish I hadn't," I told her. I didn't *mean* to be mean. Or maybe I did.

"Ophelia, being teammates is totally separate from this," she said patiently, as if she were talking to a child. "I want to be your teammate. I want to be your friend. But I just need to feel like I have a place that belongs to me, just me. I'm so sick of sharing a room, feeling like there's always somebody *there*, breathing down my neck!"

"I never breathe down your neck!" I shouted. "All I'm trying to do is live my own life. Why do you have to be such a *witch*?!"

There was a silence. "A what?" Juliet's head popped up again, over her bookcase.

"You heard me," I said.

"But did you hear *yourself*?" Juliet asked. "What did you call me?"

"I'm sorry," I replied automatically. Like I said, Juliet and I don't usually fight. I already felt bad for yelling, even though I knew I had a good reason to.

"No, don't apologize. Just say it again."

I hesitated. "Witch," I said.

"That's it!" Juliet yelled.

"That's what?" I asked. I was totally confused.

Juliet ran around the bulwark[8] she'd built, jumped onto my bed, and hugged me. "The answer to the first clue!"

---

[8]bulwark: a wall or wall-like structure built to protect or defend what's inside it.

Chapter Five

"What?"

Juliet jumped off the bed and danced around. "It's the Witch! We have to go see the Witch! Don't you get it? It *must* be her. Everybody's scared of the Witch!"

"You mean Mrs. Sparrow?" I asked.

Juliet rolled her eyes. "I guess that's her real name. You know who I mean."

I did.

The Witch was a thin, stooped old woman with long, wild gray hair. She lives a few blocks away from us on Vine Street, in a tumbledown stone house with big stone walls around it. The shingles on the roof are all covered with moss, and the yard is like a jungle, full of overgrown shrubs and weird, creeping plants. When I was younger, I'd ride by on my bike, half-hoping and half-dreading that the Witch would come out. She hardly ever showed herself, except to yell at kids who stole apples from the trees that leaned over the stone walls or tried to sneak through her yard, using it as a shortcut to the little pond in the woods where we ice-skate in winter.

The rumor was that she hated kids, and that if

she caught you she'd keep you in chains down in her cellar. I knew that was ridiculous, even when I was only seven or eight, but I still kind of enjoyed the little chill the story gave me. And who knew what she *would* do?

My parents always told us to just steer clear of the house. "If she wants to be left alone, she should be left alone," said Poppy. "She has a right to her privacy."

"I don't know," I said slowly to Juliet. "Do you really think it's her?"

Juliet ran back to her side of the room for the notebook she'd brought to the library. She flipped open to the page with the poem on it. "Look," she said excitedly. She read out loud, "'My crown of jet now gone to gray.' It's *got* to be her! You're the one who said that probably meant gray hair! Plus, the stuff about kids running and hiding from her. It's perfect!"

It wasn't much to go on. I stared down at the poem, reading to myself. *Where nightshade joins the meadow rue.* "Oh, my God!" I said suddenly. "You're right! Check it out — where does the Witch live?"

"What do you mean?" Juliet asked. "You know where she lives. Over on Buttercup Road. What does that have to do with anything?"

"Think about it," I said. "The house is on a corner. Which two streets?"

Juliet was quiet for a moment. Then she screamed. "Aaaahhhh! Vine and Buttercup!" She held up her hand for a high five.

"Shhh!" I said. "What if the twins hear you, or Katherine?"

"Katherine's out with Mom," she told me. "And the twins took off early this morning. I think they were meeting Miranda somewhere. She called and woke everybody up." Then she held up her hand again.

I smacked it. "Vine and Buttercup," I said. "Where nightshade joins the meadow rue."

We jumped up and down, doing a little victory dance around my bed. "We got it, we got it," I said. "Let's call Emma and Zoe. We have to get over there."

Juliet stopped dancing. "Oh," she said. "That's right. We have to *go* there. And *do* something. A task."

"You're not scared, are you?" I asked.

"Of course I'm not —" Juliet, always honest, stopped herself. "Yup. Aren't you?"

"Terrified," I said. "But" — I held up a finger — "remember Roosevelt's words!"

"Right." Juliet wasn't convinced. "I'll remember them when I'm locked in chains, down in the Witch's cellar."

Chapter Six

An hour later, the four of us stood on the sidewalk, two houses down from the corner of Vine and Buttercup, and stared at the Witch's house. It looked as creepy as ever. What if we were wrong about the clue? What if we were headed for the Witch's dungeon? I shook myself. No, we were right. I knew we were. "Let's go," I said.

"Do we *have* to?" asked Emma.

Emma had always been especially afraid of the Witch. She had bad dreams about her all through second grade. Even now, she'll take the long way around just to avoid passing the Witch's house. Emma's not pusillanimous[9] in general. It's just the Witch who gets to her.

Zoe nodded. "If we want to find the fortune, we do. We can't get the second clue without finishing the first one. There's a task to do, remember?"

Emma nodded. "I know it's silly," she said. "I know there's nothing to be afraid of. It's just —"

"We know," said Juliet. "It's the Witch's house."

Zoe didn't get it. I guess if I'd grown up in Penn-

[9]pusillanimous: lacking courage

sylvania instead of Cloverdale, I wouldn't get it, either. "You guys," she said impatiently, "come on! Quit stalling!" She marched up the street without looking back.

I gave Emma's hand a squeeze. "It'll be okay," I told her. "Would Grandpa Grover put us in danger?"

She shrugged. "I guess not," she said.

"Of course he wouldn't!" I tried to sound more sure than I felt. "His whole thing was about keeping kids safe, remember? I mean, he was a crossing guard!"

Emma grinned. "Remember when he'd wear that clown outfit?" she asked. "Every Halloween, he'd come out dressed in that baggy polka-dotted suit and those gigantic purple shoes —"

"And hand out Tootsie Roll pops!" I finished. "Good old Grandpa Grover."

"Come *on*!" Juliet called from up the street where she'd caught up with Zoe. She waved to us. "Katherine's team is probably *there* already!"

That did it. "Let's go, Emma. It's time." We marched up the sidewalk to where Zoe and Juliet were waiting.

The four of us looked up at the house. It was *so* creepy, like some fairy-tale witch's house in the middle of the woods.

"It's like Hansel and Gretel or something," Zoe whispered, echoing my thoughts.

"Oh, great," moaned Emma. "Now I have to think about her baking us in her oven."

Zoe sighed. "Forget I said it. Come on. I'll go first." The rusty hinges of the cast-iron gate squealed as she pushed it open. "Here goes nothing," she said, starting up the path.

I followed her, with Emma behind me and Juliet behind Emma. I knew what Juliet was thinking: Emma might run for it. We couldn't let that happen: We had to do this as a team.

We walked up the front steps, avoiding the huge cracks and the crumbling bricks. When all four of us were on the porch, Zoe nodded. "Ready?" she asked.

We were dwarfed by the big, dark door in front of us. I stared at the tarnished brass knocker in the shape of a lion's head.

Emma gulped. "R-ready," she finally said.

"Ready," Juliet and I said together.

Zoe reached up and banged the knocker. Once, twice, three times. The booming sound echoed inside.

Then there were footsteps.

Emma grabbed my sleeve. "She's coming!" she whispered.

The door opened slowly, creaking just like the gate had.

"Good morning. Mrs. Sparrow is expecting you."

Frozen in place, we stared at the man who'd opened the door. He was tall and thin and held himself as straight as an upright casket. His gray hair and gray mustache were neatly trimmed, and his extremely tasteful maroon tie set off his dark suit and white shirt. It was the kind of outfit you don't see too often in Cloverdale, Vermont. Suddenly, I had a moment of panic. Was he an undertaker? Had we gotten there too late? Was the Witch — dead?

The man just stood there, expressionless, holding the door open.

"Are you the butler?" Zoe blurted out.

Then he smiled. It was a tiny smile, about the tiniest I've ever seen, but it was definitely a smile. He shook his head. "Mrs. Sparrow does not retain a butler," he said. "May I know to whom I am speaking?" He reached into the inside pocket of his suit jacket and pulled out a tiny black notebook and a gold pen. He opened the notebook and held the pen poised above a page.

"But if you're not the butler, who are you?" Juliet asked. "I mean, if we're going to tell you who *we* are . . ."

"I am Mr. James Grover's attorney," he said. "My name is Edwin Drudge. And you are — ?"

Juliet told him. Then he turned to Zoe.

"Zoe Shapiro," Zoe said, watching as he wrote her name down. "So, you're, like, the referee for this treasure hunt? The judge?"

"Correct," he said. "I will be overseeing the treasure hunt, as per Mr. Grover's wishes." He turned to me. "May I have your name?" he asked.

Quickly, he finished taking down all of our names. "Now," he said, "may I introduce you to Mrs. Sparrow?"

We nodded, without speaking. This whole thing was just too weird. Mr. Drudge led us into the house, past a winding staircase, past dusty glass-fronted cabinets filled with strange items like African masks and carved animals, past mysterious dim hallways and tightly closed doors. The house was dark, and what little light came in from outside peeked through the heavy green brocade curtains that covered every window.

I felt Emma grab the back of my shirt. I turned to give her an encouraging smile. Then I saw her face freeze. "What's that smell?" she asked.

I sniffed. So did Juliet. Zoe was up ahead, still following Mr. Drudge. The smell was spicy, sweet. It reminded me of Christmas.

"It's — it's *gingerbread*," I said. Then I giggled.

"This really *is* just like Hansel and Gretel. Wasn't the witch's house *made* out of gingerbread?"

"Ophelia!" Emma gasped. Then she couldn't help herself. I think it was nerves that made her start giggling, too. "Maybe the roof is made out of moldy chocolate bars," she said.

I pictured the mossy shingles and cracked up.

Juliet was laughing, too. "And the stone wall is made out of gumdrops. Better watch out if she gets you near the oven," she said. "She might push you right in!"

By then we were on our way through a swinging door, following Zoe and Mr. Drudge. Our giggles stopped as we walked into a bright, clean kitchen filled with the sweet scent of baking. A gray-haired woman was leaning into the open oven. She turned, just as we came in.

It was the Witch.

But she was different. Her hair was in a neat bun. She wore a white apron embroidered with yellow flowers. And she didn't yell at us, or try to push us into the oven.

Without even consulting his notebook, Mr. Drudge introduced us, getting all of our names exactly right.

Mrs. Sparrow smiled. "Welcome," she said. "How about some gingerbread?" She held out a cookie tray.

* * *

Emma gulped and looked at me. I knew what she was thinking. What if the gingerbread was poisoned or something?

"N-no, thanks," Emma said to the Witch.

"It's not poisoned," the Witch said with a little smile.

We must have looked shocked, because she burst out laughing. "Oh, I know what you children think," she said. "But none of it is true. I'm nothing but a lonely old woman, and I'm delighted to have company." She paused. "I'd be even more delighted if you'd sit down and chat for a while," she added. "And maybe I can convince you to nibble on some of this."

"I'll have some," Juliet said bravely. She grabbed a piece of gingerbread off the cookie sheet and took a bite. "Mmm, delicious," she said.

The Witch — I mean, Mrs. Sparrow — looked very pleased. "I'm so glad you like it," she said. "Now, who will help me put this on a plate? And will one of you pour some lemonade?"

We got busy, and by the time we sat down at the kitchen table even Emma seemed more relaxed. We started to talk and ask questions, and Mrs. Sparrow ended up telling us all kinds of great stories about the old days in Cloverdale.

"Did you know that there used to be ice-skating

parties on the green?" she asked when we wondered about what kids used to do for fun. "Every winter, old Mr. Ferris would flood a section of the green with water and rig up some lights. We'd skate for hours, into the evening. Our mothers would send along thermoses of hot chocolate, and we'd sit by the bonfire and warm our toes while we drank it."

"What did you do in the summer?" asked Emma. By then she was munching away on her third piece of gingerbread.

"Oh, summer," said Mrs. Sparrow in a soft voice. Her eyes took on a distant look. "Summer was picnics and band music in the gazebo and fireworks over the fountain on the Fourth of July. Summer was peach pie and vanilla ice cream we made ourselves, cranking away out on the porch."

She even told us stories of the *way* olden days, when Cloverdale was an important stagecoach stop on the route from Montpelier (our state's capital, in case you forgot) to Burlington. Anyway, it all sounded so cool. People used to *do* things together in this town. I almost wished I'd been born fifty years ago. Cloverdale's nothing like that now.

It turned out that the poem was right about the Witch. The only thing we had to fear was fear itself. Mrs. Sparrow was friendly and sweet and easy to talk to. She'd been a kindergarten teacher in town until she married, so I guess she didn't hate children after all. Maybe she was just like Juliet, someone who needed her "personal space." Anyway, it was clear that all those stories were just that: stories. Mrs. Sparrow was sweet and kind and maybe more than a little lonely. She'd been living alone in that house for over ten years, ever since her husband died.

She showed us a picture of herself with her last kindergarten class. "This is the last photograph of me as Miss Rose," she said, pointing to a pretty, young black-haired girl surrounded by children. They stood in front of the old school, a big red brick building that's now a home for older women. I can see that building from my house, so I recognized it right away.

"Miss Rose!" I said. "And now Mrs. Sparrow. Sparrow, like a bird. 'A Blossom once, a Bird today.' I get it!"

She smiled at me. "Very good," she said.

It felt great to have solved the first clue. Then I remembered something. "But what about the task?" I asked. "Isn't there something we're supposed to do?"

Mrs. Sparrow looked at Mr. Drudge, who had been sitting there quietly the whole time, his back straight and his hands on his knees. He produced another small notebook, checked a list, and nodded to himself. "You can rake leaves, pull weeds, dust the parlor, or tidy the basement," he said. "Your choice. The first team here cleaned out the attic, and the second washed these windows." He gestured at the kitchen windows.

"Such nice young people," murmured Mrs. Sparrow. "It's been so hard to keep up with things since Mr. Sparrow passed away."

"You mean —" I couldn't believe my ears. *First team,* he'd said. *Second team.* "We're not the first?"

"Oh, no," said Mrs. Sparrow. "But don't you worry. Everybody who finds their way here will get the second clue."

I'd almost forgotten.

"The second clue!" said Zoe eagerly. "What is it?"

Mr. Drudge cleared his throat. "After you complete the task," he said.

Chapter Seven

We decided to rake leaves, since it was that rare thing: a nice November day. We figured we might as well be outside. I don't mind raking, which is a good thing since we have so many trees in our yard at home. When I was little, I used to love jumping into leaf piles. I probably drove my parents nuts, blasting apart the careful piles they'd made. But that day, we just got down to business. The Witch's — I mean, Mrs. Sparrow's — yard probably hadn't been raked in a few years; it took us an hour of hard work just to clear the part in front of the house. My hands were blistered and I felt all sweaty and dusty, but I didn't really care. This may sound dopey, but it felt good to be helping Mrs. Sparrow.

It felt even better to see Katherine and her entourage[10] show up late. "Finally figured it out, huh?" I asked, loving the look on her face when she spotted me.

[10]entourage: a group of followers who hang around waiting to serve an important person

She didn't answer, just tossed her head and led the boys up to the door.

Juliet and I exchanged a grin. "Yesss," I whispered.

"But we weren't first," Emma reminded us, leaning on her rake. "We're going to have to work harder if we want to find the treasure."

After a little while, Mr. Drudge brought Katherine and the boys outside and showed them where to pull weeds. Then he looked at the area we'd raked, told us that we'd completed our task, and invited us back inside to get the next clue. Katherine shot me a nasty look as I passed her.

Back in the kitchen, we nibbled on more gingerbread while Mrs. Sparrow gave us the next clue. She stood with hands clasped in front of her and her eyes closed, reciting the clue:

"Beside the Stage (capital S), a shell of red,
Once home to books and social pleasures.
Inside: a stage, with veil of red,
Now home to dusty ancient treasures.
The young have grown and fled the nest,
The souls here now have come to rest.
Your task:
You'll find the third clue on the day
That sleeping horses spout and spray."

We all listened carefully. It sounded just as con-fusing as the first clue, but maybe it wouldn't be as hard, now that we knew what we were doing.

She opened her eyes and smiled. "Now, say it back to me," she urged.

"Beside the Stage, a shell of red, once . . ." I stumbled after the first line.

"Once home to books and social pleasures," she offered.

"Right." I tried the third and fourth lines. "In-side there's a stage with a red veil . . . No, that won't work." I tried again. "Inside: a stage, with veil of red . . ." I finished the poem, messing it up but finally getting to the end.

"Excellent. Now say it again."

This time Zoe tried and got it right on the first try.

Juliet, meanwhile, had fished her notebook out of her backpack and was busy writing it down.

"Well, dears, I wish you luck!" said Mrs. Spar-row, seeing us off. "Come back and visit anytime."

We promised we would, and I, for one, really meant it. I'd enjoyed her stories about the past and wanted to hear more. And the gingerbread wasn't bad, either.

We waved at Katherine as we left. She didn't seem to be doing much weeding; it was more like

she was supervising the boys. "See you when —
or should I say *if*? — you solve the next one!" I
called to her as we let ourselves out through the
gate. She just glared at me.

The four of us walked along, reciting the clue
over and over. "A shell of red," mused Zoe. "What
could that mean?"

"Somebody who wears red all the time?" Emma
suggested. "Like a firefighter? Or maybe it means
a red building."

"That's good!" I said. "I like that."

"And there's another thing about it being beside
the Stage," Juliet said. "That sounds like the name
of a river, maybe. Or a road?"

"I don't know anything by that name in this
town," I said. "At least, I don't think so. We can
look at the town map, back at our house."

Mom loves maps of every type, so the walls of
the study upstairs are practically covered in them.
There are old maps and new maps, maps that show
geological features, maps of Europe and Africa and
Antarctica. And maps of Cloverdale and the area
around it. The nicest one of those is a hand-drawn
map of the town that shows all the landmarks and
road names. As soon as we got home we went
straight over and examined it carefully.

"I don't see any Stage River, or Stage Road,"
said Zoe. "I guess it's not in Cloverdale."

"Maybe it's not even real," Emma suggested. "Maybe it's a made-up name, from a book or something."

"Or maybe it's not a road or a river at all," said Juliet. She threw her notebook onto the floor in disgust.

Zoe plopped down into one of the old armchairs. I sat down on the rug at her feet, rubbing Bob's ears. He'd followed us into the study, hoping for attention.

"Face it, it could mean *anything*," I said. I picked up Juliet's notebook and read the clue again. "Now, this stuff about horses makes it sound like a farm."

"There aren't too many farms around here anymore," Emma pointed out.

"So maybe it *used* to be a farm," Juliet said. "Like the Cloverdale Inn. That used to be a farm. Now it's a bed-and-breakfast. We should go there and check it out."

"Wait, though." I tapped my pencil against my teeth. "Do souls rest at a farm?" I pointed to a line in the clue.

"Maybe there's a cemetery nearby," said Juliet.

We didn't talk about it too much longer. It was getting late, and we all had homework to finish for Monday morning. Juliet typed the clue into our computer and printed out copies for everyone, and Emma and Zoe headed home for dinner.

Katherine was setting the table when I came downstairs. "Wow! You got all that weeding done already?" I asked her. I couldn't help rubbing it in.

"Ha-ha," she said. "You know, you think you're cool just because you got there before me. Well, guess who was on the *first* team to solve the clue?" She nodded toward the kitchen, where Helena and Viola were helping Mom make dinner.

"You're kidding!" I exclaimed. "The twins?"

"I don't know how they did it, but I think we'd both better keep an eye on them." She straightened a place mat and put down the last fork.

Dinner was pretty quiet that night. After we'd each taken a turn telling something about our day — we mostly stuck to neutral topics — Mom kept asking questions about our search for the fortune. But nobody wanted to say much in case they gave something away to an opposing team.

Later, I spent a long time in the study. We're supposed to do homework in our rooms and only use the computer in the study for e-mail and research, but I didn't much feel like being in a room I barely recognized. I figured I'd let Juliet have her "space."

TO: DParker

From: WrrdGrrl

Subject: Witch no more

Well, today I learned something new about somebody old. Remember that lady we call the Witch? She's not so bad, after all. But, speaking of Witches, it's going to take some magic to solve this next clue. . . .

Chapter Eight

At school on Monday, all the Cloverdale kids were talking about the hidden fortune. U-28 is the middle and high school for lots of smaller towns that only have elementary schools, so lots of kids aren't even eligible for the contest. Everybody had heard about it, but only the Cloverdale kids were obsessing about it. Mrs. Sparrow must have had a *lot* of company the day before! Just about everybody from town was on a team — and nobody could figure out a thing about the second clue.

At least, that's what I thought. Until I overheard Katherine talking to Pete Pelkey by the second-floor water fountain.

Here's how it happened. It was between periods, so of course the halls were packed. I had just stopped at my locker and I was on my way to math when I (and fifty-six other people) passed Katherine and Pete. They were so involved in their conversation that I was pretty sure she didn't see me. In the midst of all the noise, I picked up on the sound of her voice — I guess because it's so familiar to me.

". . . Second clue's in the bag!" I heard her say. Quickly, I ducked around the corner and flattened myself against some ninth-graders' lockers. From there, I could hear perfectly without being seen. I knew it wasn't right to eavesdrop, but how could I resist?

". . . the old Cooper place. No question! It has to be the answer," Katherine was saying.

"How can you be sure?" Pete asked.

"Ryan told me that his grandfather told *him* that they used to have a little stage in their barn. They used to put on plays there, and everybody in town came. To their red barn, where the horses used to live. Get it? A shell of red?"

Pete gave a low whistle. "Got it," he said. "Great work. We'll go up there after school. Bet we'll be the first ones."

Bet again, Pete.

Was it right to steal Katherine's solution to the clue? Probably not. Was I going to do it anyway? Take a guess.

Chapter Nine

"Ophelia, this is ridiculous!" Zoe complained. "Are you *sure* about what she said?"

We were riding our bikes up Brookside Road. I'd assembled my team as quickly as possible after school. If we wanted to beat Katherine to the second clue we were going to have to move it. That meant bikes instead of walking, even if it *was* kind of drizzly. And a little chilly.

The fact was, it was miserable out. A total November experience. Rainwater was already running down inside my bike helmet. My gloves were wet and my wool socks were soaked. I had on so many layers that I could barely move, and I still wasn't warm.

"I'm sure," I answered, huffing a little. Like many of the roads in Cloverdale, Brookside is a long, steep climb. But I knew it would all be worth it when we got to the old Cooper farm at the top. Mr. Drudge was probably already there, just waiting for the early birds who were the first to figure out the clue. I imagined there might be snacks again, like there were at Mrs. Sparrow's. Some hot chocolate would hit the spot. And maybe some oatmeal-raisin cookies. I couldn't quite figure out how all the parts of the clue were going to come together, but I knew it would happen somehow.

"I can't see a thing," Emma whined. "My glasses are all fogged up."

"We're almost there," I told her. "I know exactly where this farm is. Juliet, remember when Poppy used to bring us up here in the spring, to see the baby lambs?"

Juliet just grunted at me. Rainwater was dripping off her nose.

"Here we are!" I said, turning my bike into a long gravel driveway. I rode toward the yellow farmhouse set back from the road. There was a big red barn tucked behind it. This was the place!

The farm seemed quiet. Very quiet. But there was one car in the driveway. Probably Mr. Drudge's.

I got off my bike and leaned it against the porch. Taking off my helmet, I told my teammates to wait. "I'll just check to make sure it's okay to go into the barn," I said confidently.

I knocked on the front door.

And waited.

Knocked again.

Nothing.

I looked back at the others with a weak smile. Then the door opened. "Can I help you?" asked the red-haired woman who was standing there, wiping her hands on a blue dish towel. She looked bewildered.

"It's about the clue. We figured it out. Is Mr. Drudge here?" I asked, my words tumbling over one another.

"Clue? Mr. Drudge?" She shook her head. "I'm not sure I know what you're talking about."

"This is the Cooper place, right?" I asked.

She nodded. "Sure. At least, it used to be. We bought it from Duane Cooper six years ago. He moved over to his parents' farm, over on East Hill Road."

I gulped. "Do you happen to know if his parents' farm has a big red barn?" I asked.

She thought for a second. "Why, yes, I suppose it does," she told me. "Now, you and your friends must be freezing. Would you like to come in and warm up?"

It was tempting. But we had a clue to solve. "No, thanks," I said. "Sorry to bother you!" I put my helmet back on and grabbed my bike. "Okay, guys," I said. "You heard, right? We have to go over to East Hill."

"Ugh," Juliet groaned. "All the way back down Brookside Road and back up East Hill? In this rain?"

"Look, do you want to get there first or not?" I

asked. "I bet we can still beat Katherine's team if we hurry."

That was enough to convince Juliet. She swung a leg back over her bike and got ready to go.

Emma and Zoe exchanged a look. "Okay," they both said.

We headed back down the road. If anything, it was colder going downhill. At least we'd been working hard when we were riding *up* the hill. Now we were just coasting into the rain and wind. My hands turned into icicles and the wind made my eyes water like crazy, so I could hardly see.

It took a while to climb up East Hill, but we finally made it. Guess what. The barn at *that* Cooper place wasn't red, it was gray. Mr. Drudge wasn't waiting for us. And, needless to say, neither was any hot chocolate. Instead, there was just a mean old spotted dog that chased us and a hired hand who told us that the Cooper place we were looking for was probably the one back down the hill, over behind the gravel pit.

By the time we got to *that* Cooper place, all four of us were disgusted, soaked, and not too surprised to find a new-looking ranch house with no barn and nobody home.

When we walked into the kitchen back at home, a dry, happy Katherine was waiting. "Gotcha!" she crowed when she saw me. "I *knew* you were listening! Ha! Next time, maybe you won't be so smug about getting a clue before me!"

I stood there like a dripping tatterdemalion[11]. I was cold, soaked, and ripping mad. But it would all be worth it in the end — if we found the fortune.

[11]tatterdemalion: a person dressed in rags; a ragamuffin

Chapter Ten

"Hey, Ophelia! What's new up at the old Cooper place?" Peter Brown grinned at me as he passed by my locker.

Michael Stebbins came up next to me as I walked down the hall. "Find any horses in that barn?" he asked casually.

Even Bradley White got into the act. "Nice day for a bike ride, wasn't it?" he asked as we stood in line for pizza, green salad, and canned peaches.

That one made me blush. Actually, almost anything Bradley says to me seems to make me blush these days. It's not like he's my *crush* or anything. Zoe and Emma and I have kind of pledged to wait until at least eighth grade before we start going nuts about boys. We've seen what it can do to girls' brains. Not that it's hurt Katherine much. Somehow, she manages to retain full brainpower no matter what.

I tried to ignore all the comments, but it wasn't easy. By the time homeroom ended on Tuesday, it seemed like every single person at school had heard about my team's wild-goose chase. (News travels fast at U-28, especially if Katherine's spreading it. She knows *everybody*.) And every single person had something to say about it.

I nodded and smiled and tried to act as if the teasing wasn't getting to me, but it was. Now, more than ever, I knew what I had done was wrong. I probably deserved to suffer for it. Because of me, my team had wasted an entire afternoon roaming all over the countryside in the rain. Even though I let her take the first shower when we got home, Juliet was mad enough to pretty much avoid speaking to me for the rest of the night, and Katherine never stopped gloating.

By breakfast time, Juliet had forgiven me and we'd made a plan for our team to meet at the library after we all got out of school, but Katherine was still acting smug. She just shrugged mysteriously when I asked whether her team had gotten anywhere with the clue.

Then she went and told everybody, and the teasing started.

"Don't listen to them," said Emma loyally. We were at our usual table in the cafeteria, along with Zoe. The three of us are lucky to have the same lunch period this year; last year we all ate at different times. They'd heard Bradley teasing me, and both of them had been getting comments, too. They were trying to make me feel better about the whole thing.

"Any one of them would have — hold on, I have to sneeze." Emma held up a hand and made a funny face, then let loose with a huge sternutation[12]. "Any one of them would have done the same thing," she finished, reaching into her backpack for a tissue. She sneezed again, then blew her nose.

I looked at her guiltily. "Did you catch a cold yesterday?" I asked, feeling even worse.

She stifled a third sneeze. "No. Well, maybe. But it's not your fault!"

"I should have known better," I said, shaking my head. "I should have known it was a trick."

"Forget it," Zoe said. "The important thing is to move on." She shoved her tray away and pulled out the printed copy of the clue that Juliet had given her. It was covered with penciled notes and cross-outs. Some words were circled, and others were underlined. "I know we shouldn't talk about it without Juliet here, but this is driving me crazy! I looked this over some more last night, but I didn't get anywhere. It makes even less sense than the first clue did."

"I don't know," said Emma. She took out *her* copy, which also had scribbles all over it. "At least this time we can be fairly sure it's a place, not a person. I started to make a list of all the red build-

[12]sternutation: a sneeze, or the act of sneezing

ings I could think of, like the Andersons' house, the fire station, and that old garage on Route 20."

Cloverdale is not a big town, but it's spread out. The very center of town is the village green, which is a big square area with grass and trees, patches of overgrown weeds, and the old, tumbledown gazebo where Mrs. Sparrow said there used to be concerts in the summer. My house is on Spring Street, which goes along the west side of the green. Directly across the green from us is East Street, which turns into East Hill Road as it climbs out of town. (Most of the roads out of Cloverdale go uphill, since we're in a little valley.) The northern side of the green is Route 20, which is the road that goes to Burlington, where Olivia lives. There are cool stores in Burlington and lots of good restaurants (not that my family eats out much). There's no real restaurant in Cloverdale, unless you count the sandwich cooler at the gas station minimart, where all the Cloverdale kids go to buy junk food and candy. There's not much else in the way of shopping. There are a few little stores along East Street: a dusty old general store and a health-food place, but nobody shops there much since the big Price Chopper supermarket opened a couple of miles outside of town, just past my school.

There are other houses on the streets that branch off from the main ones that surround the green, and lots of old and new buildings and businesses strung out along Route 20. Zoe and her brother and her mom — her parents are divorced — live in a building that used to be a mill, out by Tucker's Creek, and Emma and her parents — she's an only child — live over by the elementary school and the library, in a newer development called Cloverdale Terrace.

I tried to think of some more red buildings, but it wasn't easy. "What about the feed store?" I asked. That's out past the garage. "It's red. Maybe that would tie in with the horse thing in the clue."

"The feed store?" Zoe shook her head. "That just doesn't seem right."

Emma didn't say anything. She just sneezed again.

Just then, the bell rang. Lunch period was over and I'd barely eaten. I gobbled my pizza down quickly, washing it down with chocolate milk. "We'll figure it out," I said as I took the last bite. I was trying to sound confident, but so far, this clue had me stumped.

There were three other teams working at the library later that afternoon. At least we weren't the only ones who found the clue abstruse[13]. I saw He-

---

[13]abstruse: difficult to understand

lena and Viola and their friends over in the Vermont section, poring over old books. I felt a little better knowing that they were still puzzling over the clue.

"Okay," said Juliet. "Here's what I think. We have to figure out this stage thing. That's for sure." We had spread out around one of the tables in the reference area, each of us with her own copy of the clue in front of her.

"You mean the first time it says stage, where it's capitalized, or the second time?" asked Emma.

"Both," Juliet answered. "We have to figure out *where* Stage is, since that will give us a location. And we have to figure out what the other stage means. It does sound like a place where plays were put on. But where could that be?"

"Okay, let's start with the first Stage," suggested Zoe. "I think we should look at some old maps. Maybe there's something that *used* to be called Stage." She pushed back her chair and headed for the Vermont section, too antsy to sit still any longer. Juliet was right behind her.

"I'm working on this part in the middle," Emma told me while we waited for the others, "the part about how the young have grown and fled the nest. Could that have something to do with birds? Like, the pigeons that live in that old gazebo on the green?" She sneezed, then frowned down at her paper.

"I don't know," I said. "This part about horses is what I'm most curious about. Since when do horses spray and spout? I've only heard them whinnying and neighing." Mom has a friend who lives on a horse farm in the next town over. Sometimes I go there with her and bring carrots and apples for the horses. Their teeth are huge and the crunching noises they make are so loud, but I hold the food out on my flat palm and I've never even been nipped. They're all trained to take treats gently.

"Yes!"

"We got it!"

Zoe's voice rang from across the room, interrupting my drifting train of thought. She was high-fiving Juliet as both of them looked down at a map they'd spread out on a table. I saw Helena and Viola run over to see what they'd found. I also saw Ms. Rosoff look in their direction. Any minute she was going to tell them to quiet down.

"You guys," I hissed, waving to them. "Bring it over here!"

Juliet pulled the map away from Helena, who was trying to grab it, and came back to our table. "Look!" she whispered, pointing to a spot on the map.

"It's Stage Road!" Zoe whispered, not quite as softly. Zoe has a hard time being quiet.

I stared at the map. I saw Stage Road, but I couldn't figure out how it fit into my idea of Cloverdale — the Cloverdale of now, instead of the Cloverdale of 1937. That was the date on the map.

"Route 20!" said Emma suddenly. "Stage Road is Route 20!" She pointed to four roads that made a square. "See? That's the green, in the middle. There's Spring Street. I bet that little mark is your house!"

That's when I got it. I smacked myself on the forehead. "Stage Road, like a stagecoach!" I said.

"Shhh!" Juliet said. "Look who's coming."

It was Helena and Viola. "Can we see?" Helena asked. "Come on, show us what you found. We know you found something!"

Juliet flipped the map over.

"We have something, too!" Viola said teasingly.

"Want to trade?" asked Helena. "You tell us what you figured out, and we'll tell you."

My teammates and I looked at one another. I saw Zoe nod, then Emma. Juliet was last, but finally she nodded, too.

"Okay," I said. "Here's what we have." I turned the map faceup again. "Stage Road is the same as Route 20."

Viola grinned. "Excellent," she said. "Old maps — what a great idea! We've been looking at this book, *Historical Theatres and Other Landmarks in Vermont*."

"And?" I prompted.

"And what?" she asked, avoiding my eyes.

"What did you find?" I asked. I was starting to get a bad feeling.

"Well, it's not as good as yours," Viola began.

"It's not really too good at all," Helena said, not sounding very sorry. "But we'll tell you. The only thing we could find about a stage — you know, the other kind? — was in that book. It talks about Cloverdale having an opera house."

"An *opera* house?" Zoe asked.

"Lots of towns had them," Viola said. "It was just a fancy name for a big auditorium where people could see plays or music."

"But that's perfect!" I said. "I bet it had red curtains and everything!" I was thinking of that "veil of red" line.

"Maybe it did," Helena said. "But we'll never find out. It burned down in nineteen-thirty-two."

Emma stared at her. "So, what you're saying is, you didn't really find an answer at all!"

"And we can't go there, because it doesn't exist," Zoe added.

Viola nodded, a little shamefaced.

Helena shrugged. "Oh, well!" She grinned at us, shrugging. "Thanks for the help!" She and Viola took off, leaving us a little stunned.

We sat back down at our table. Nobody spoke for a few moments.

"Now what?" Emma asked finally.

Juliet smacked a hand on the table. "If it's not in the history books, maybe we can find out from a person. A person who lived in town back then!"

"Like who?" I asked. Then I caught her eye, and I knew what she was thinking. "Mrs. Sparrow!" I jumped to my feet. "Let's go."

Chapter Eleven

The house and yard looked completely different. Everything was neat and tidy: no weeds, no leaves, no climbing vines all over the trees. Mrs. Sparrow answered the door herself this time, smiling. She was wearing a blue apron, embroidered with green flowers. "Well, well," she said. "Come in! More company. You'll have to remind me of your names. I've had so many visitors, I can't keep track!"

We reintroduced ourselves, and she invited us back into the kitchen. We walked through the house, which was much less dark and dusty than it had been just two days before. Even the heavy curtains had been pulled back to let in more light.

"I just started making a pie," said Mrs. Sparrow. "Would you like to help?"

We all said we would, so she assigned jobs. Zoe and I were to peel apples, and Emma was to cut them into pieces. "And you, Miss Juliet," said Mrs. Sparrow, "can help me roll out the dough."

"Now, then," she said when we were all working away. "Did you have some questions for me?"

"How did you know?" I asked.

She smiled. "Well, for one thing, I gave you a very difficult clue the other day. And for another, I've had several young people come by to talk to me since then."

"So it's okay to ask your help?" Zoe asked, dropping an apple peel onto the floor. She bent to pick it up.

"Of course," said Mrs. Sparrow. "I'll answer any questions you ask. People don't learn about history just from books, you know. The only thing I won't do is *tell* you the answer. One young lady seemed to think I would, but I set her straight."

I pictured Katherine stomping down the porch stairs. I bet it was her.

I finished peeling one apple and picked up another, thinking. "Okay," I said. "Here's a question. Where did people used to get together for 'social pleasures'?"

"That's easy," said Mrs. Sparrow, dusting some flour from her hands. "The green. It used to be such a gathering place, with the weekly concerts at the gazebo and the picnics near the fountain —" She had a faraway look in her eyes, and I hated to interrupt. But I was too impatient not to.

"I mean, in winter," I corrected myself. "Where did they go in winter? Maybe someplace that had a stage? With red curtains?"

She nodded. "Good question," she said. "I believe you're thinking of the old opera house."

Emma laughed. "You can't trick us," she said. "We know that burned down. But there must have been *another* stage in town. One that wouldn't be in the history books."

Mrs. Sparrow turned and put her hands on her hips. "Well, there was the auditorium where my students and I used to put on plays," she said slowly.

"At the school?" I asked. All I could picture was the boring multipurpose room at the elementary school. It has no red curtains, no stage. And it always smells like a gym.

Then I remembered the picture of Miss Rose and her class. "The *old* school!" I said. "The brick one!"

"Brick is red!" chimed in Emma. "Why didn't we *think* of that? A shell of *red*!"

"'The young have grown and fled the nest,'" quoted Juliet. "That's the kids. They've graduated!"

"And the souls that are resting are the old people who live there now!" finished Zoe. "That's it! We've got it!"

Mrs. Sparrow just smiled. "You're the first," she said. "You asked the right questions. Yes, that building was a real gathering place, back when it was the only school in town. Now that the children are all over in that new building, and the older ones are clear out of town, it's just not the same." She sighed.

Yahoo! We were first. I wanted to run right over to the old school that minute. It's kitty-corner across the green from my house! I've probably seen it every single day of my life. I couldn't believe I hadn't thought of it. I guess knowing that Route 20 and Stage Road were the same made a big difference.

But I didn't run. We'd said we would help with the pie, and we did. By the time we got it into the oven, it was nearly dark, and time for us to head home. We were going to have to wait until after school the next day to explore the "dusty treasures" and figure out our next task.

Chapter Twelve

On the way home, Juliet and I agreed to play it cool so that Katherine, Helena, and Viola wouldn't know we had solved the clue. I'd learned my lesson about gloating. Besides, we couldn't be *positive* we were right until we'd been to the school. And we still didn't know what the task was.

Miranda's car was in the driveway when we got there. No surprise. She comes to dinner at least a couple of times a week, sometimes with her fiancé, Steve. But it *was* a surprise to see Olivia's little red car, too. Unlike Miranda, who's still really attached to our house and our parents and the whole Parker gestalt[14], Olivia keeps herself more separate. She drops by now and then, but she's mostly pretty involved with her life up in Burlington. Besides studying photography, she works as a waitress at this cool restaurant that's like a fifties diner. She's been on her own for a couple of years already; she left home when she was seventeen.

I don't think it's any secret that I'm Olivia's favorite sister and she's mine. We have a certain

[14]gestalt: a whole that can't be separated into or described by its parts

79

bond that goes beyond what I have with any of my other sisters. She always makes me feel special.

"Hey!" she said when I walked into the kitchen. She had her hands in the big brown mixing bowl, mushing stuff around. I would have been grossed out, except that I knew right away that she was making meatballs, her specialty. Bob was lurking around, hoping for scraps the way he always does when somebody's cooking. He's always there to scarf up anything that falls on the floor. Olivia held up her hands, all dripping with yucky, eggy hamburger. "I'd hug you, but —" she said.

I backed away, holding up my hands. "No thanks!" We grinned at each other.

"Want any help?" I asked. "Where's Mom? Where's everybody?"

"Not unless you've already done your homework, in the study, and who can keep track?" Olivia answered my questions in order. "So, how's the treasure hunt going?"

"Great!" I said. Then I caught myself. Somebody might be listening. "I mean, okay. The second clue is really hard. But I bet my team will solve it soon," I said carefully.

Olivia gave me a funny look. She knows me so well. She could tell I wasn't exactly telling the truth.

I grabbed a pad from the kitchen counter and

scribbled a note on it, then held it out so she could see.

She read it, nodded, and gave me a huge smile and two greasy, hamburger-y thumbs-up. "Well, just keep working on it," she said out loud. "I'm sure you'll get it soon enough." She winked at me. "Now go on and get your homework done so we can hang out after dinner."

I heard voices from the living room: Helena's first, then Viola's. Miranda was talking, too. But when I passed through on my way upstairs, Helena and Viola were just leaving. Miranda was sitting alone on the couch, looking through an old photo album, the one with the used-to-be-white satin cover, where all our baby pictures are kept. Or, should I say, *her* baby pictures. By the time I came along, Mom and Poppy didn't bother to drag out the camera every time a kid smiled or burped.

"Steve and I thought it might be fun to have our baby pictures on the invitations for our rehearsal dinner," she said. Miranda's been planning every detail of her wedding ever since Steve slipped the ring on her finger. Every detail, that is, except the date. I think she actually enjoys the planning more than anything, so she keeps putting the *actual* wedding off. Right now they're talking about the August after next.

She's already decided about her flowers down

to the last daisy, what her bridesmaids will wear (as one of them, can I just say, *Yuck*), and exactly what shade of pink the tablecloths will be. She knows precisely how many guests they'll have, and how many of them will prefer chicken over salmon. And now she was planning the invitations to the rehearsal dinner!

"I always liked the one where you look like E.T.," I said.

She reached out to give me a playful smack. "If you *ever* show that picture to Steve, I will personally —" I didn't wait to hear the rest. I dodged her hand and ran up the stairs, laughing.

Juliet was at her desk when I walked into our room. It was funny; I was already getting used to the new arrangement in there. At least, my stomach didn't do a total flip anymore when I first came in. It was still a little weird that I couldn't see her when I was lying down, but I could live with that. "Meatballs for dinner!" I said, tossing my backpack onto my bed. I'd forgotten to make it that morning, so Doogey was peeking out from a mound of blankets and pillows (I have three, including the one that goes over my head), and Jenny was snuggled in like a hen in a nest.

"Mmm-hmm." Juliet didn't look up.

"Thought you loved them," I said. "You're always begging Olivia to make them when she's here."

"Mmm-hmm." This time, she shifted her chair a little so her back was more toward me.

"Can you believe Miranda and her wedding?" I unzipped my backpack so I could start unloading stuff from school. "Now she's planning the rehearsal dinner invitations."

No answer.

"Have you talked to the twins?" I asked, pulling out my math book. Ugh. I had *tons* of problems to do that night. "Or Katherine? I wonder if they got anywhere with the clue today. I bet not. I bet we're the only ones who —"

Juliet moved her chair again. This time there was just something *about* that little movement. I stopped in midsentence.

"Juliet?"

No answer.

"Are you — what, are you mad at me or something?"

She turned around in her chair. No smile. "No," she said, in this patient I'm-speaking-to-an-idiot tone of voice. "I'm not mad. I just don't want to chat all the time. Not when we're in here." She waved a hand around at the room. "Don't you get it?"

Suddenly, I had this huge lump in my throat. "No," I said quietly. "No, I guess I don't." I really didn't. Just minutes ago, we'd walked home together, all excited about what a great team we had. All afternoon, she'd been acting just the way she always did. We were pals. Teammates. But now that we were back in our room, she was pushing me away again. It was like Dr. Juliet and Mr. Snide.

I stuck my math book back into my pack and walked out.

The study was empty, and I was glad. I didn't feel like talking to anyone just then. I plopped down in the desk chair and turned on the computer. Might as well check my e-mail, as long as I was banned from my own room.

I know, I know. She didn't *ban* me. But that's what it felt like.

I typed in my screen name and password. Nothing from Poppy. Boo. But the word of the day was a good one: *imbroglio*, meaning a confused or difficult situation. How appropriate. And there was a long note from my friend Amanda, who moved to Connecticut with her mom when her parents split up. Amanda's been pretty unhappy lately, and I never know exactly how to help. Mostly I just write back and tell her how much I miss her and that she'll always be my friend. I was reading her note when the voice said, "You've got mail" again.

I clicked on new mail — and there was a note from Poppy! That meant he was on-line right that minute. I didn't even stop to read his letter: Instead, I clicked on instant message. POPPY! I typed in. ARE YOU THERE?

A second later, I got a reply. I SURE AM, it said.

YAY! I wrote. I MISS YOU!

MISS YOU, TOO, SUGARBUMP, he wrote. WHAT'S NEW WITH YOU? FOUND THAT FORTUNE YET?

STILL WORKING ON IT. IT'S FUN. BUT JULIET'S BEING A PILL. I realized I hadn't really talked to Poppy about the whole situation yet. SHE WANTS HER 'PERSONAL SPACE.'

DON'T WE ALL? Poppy typed back.

NO! I wrote. I DON'T. I JUST WANT THINGS TO BE THE WAY THEY USED TO BE.

HAVE YOU TALKED TO HER?

TRIED TO. BUT IT'S LIKE WE'RE SPEAKING DIFFERENT LANGUAGES.

SOUNDS LIKE TIME FOR A FAMILY MEETING, Poppy typed back.

WITHOUT YOU?

He typed in a frowny face. WISH I COULD BE THERE. HEY. I HAVE TO GO. LOVE YOU! THINK ABOUT THIS: THE ROOM UNDER THE ATTIC STAIRS.

WHAT? I typed back. THE JUNK ROOM?

But there was no answer. He must have signed off.

I sat there thinking for a minute. Then I signed off, too, and went to find Mom.

Family meetings at the Parker house can be a really big deal. Or not. Sometimes we have them just for fun, like if we want to talk about how we're going to decorate the Christmas tree that year. Sometimes they're boring: Somebody wants to talk *again* about the way we assign chores. And sometimes they're very, very interesting.

That night's meeting fell into the last category. Some stuff came out that I never knew before.

We were in the living room, after dinner. Helena and Viola had claimed the couch; they lay with their heads at either end and their legs all tangled up together. Charles the cat crouched on the back of the couch, dipping a paw down occasionally to bat at Helena's hair. Bob was sprawled out next to Miranda, who was on the floor, still leafing through photo albums. A bunch of them were spread out on the dark green carpet around her. Mom grabbed the recliner Poppy usually sits in, Katherine lounged on the love seat, and Olivia and I squished into the oversized easy chair together, me with Jenny curled up in my lap. Juliet sat in the rocking chair, which is nearest to the arched doorway into the hall where the stairs are. It was almost as if she wanted to be ready to bolt.

"Okay, Ophelia, you're on," said Mom. "What's the issue?"

"Juliet," I said. "She hates me."

"Oh, please!" Juliet got halfway out of the rocking chair. See? She wanted to leave.

"Juliet, sit tight," said Mom. "We know you don't hate your sister. But obviously she's getting *some* kind of bad vibe from you."

Olivia nudged me and snickered. We get a kick out of it when Mom and Poppy use those sixties expressions. But this time, I couldn't even fake a giggle.

"So, why don't you each tell your side of the story?" Miranda suggested. "Ophelia, you go first, since you called the meeting."

So I told about how Juliet was acting like our room only belonged to her, and how she wouldn't talk to me when we were in there together, and how it felt like she was shoving me away. I had a lump in my throat the whole time, but I managed not to cry.

Then Juliet had her turn. She was all "blah, blah, blah, need my space, she shouldn't take it personally, blah, blah, blah." Same old stuff. I turned to Olivia and rolled my eyes. But she wasn't looking at me. She was looking at Juliet — and nodding.

"I know exactly what you mean," Olivia said. "I felt that way the whole time I was twelve. Miranda would come into our room and say two words to me and I'd want to scream!"

"Sometimes you *did*," Miranda said. She looked up at me from her spot on the floor. "Ophelia, I can relate to what you're going through. That year with Olivia was the worst. She got over it after a while, if that's any help."

"*I* never did," Mom spoke up, very quietly.

We all turned to look at her. "What do you mean?" I asked.

"I always hated sharing a room," she answered. "Always. I loved my sisters. I adored them. But I couldn't stand being forced to *live* with them. It was pure torture. The happiest day of my life was when I got my first single dorm room at college. That was the first room I didn't have to share. It was heaven."

I was speechless. This was a whole new side of Mom. But it opened up a whole interesting discussion of how everyone's different. Helena and Viola, of course, didn't have a clue about what Olivia, Mom, and Juliet were talking about. They're *always* together, and they like it that way. Katherine mostly listened with this smug look on her face: She's happy because she knows nobody wants to share a room with *her*, so her personal space is safe.

We talked for a long time, and I guess I felt a tiny

bit better once I understood a little more about how Juliet was feeling. But something still had to change. It was time to bring up Poppy's idea. "What about if one of us moves into the junk room?" I proposed.

"Are you joking?" Mom asked. "Nobody could live in there. It's way too small! And it's full of — well, *junk*!"

She was right. The room is a tiny, windowless cube, more like a closet. And it's packed with boxes and tons of stuff we never use but may want someday.

"We can clean it out," I said. "And all that has to go in there is a bed and maybe a chair. I could use the desk in the study and still keep my clothes in our old room."

"*Your* clothes?" asked Juliet. "What do you mean? *You're* going to move?"

I nodded. It was as if I'd made the decision while I was talking. If Juliet moved out, leaving me abandoned in the room we'd shared, I'd feel even worse about the situation. If someone was going to leave, it was going to be me. I'd clear out and give Juliet her space. Maybe I'd discover that *I* liked having space, too. Maybe I'd learn all kinds of new things about myself, living alone.

"Yup," I said. "I'm going to move."

Chapter Thirteen

We agreed that I'd make the big move on Saturday, since there wouldn't be time during the rest of the week. After our meeting, I sent an e-mail to Poppy, thanking him for the great idea. Later, when we were getting ready for bed, Juliet actually spoke to me. "Thanks," she said as she pulled out her clothes for the next day (Juliet's very organized that way). "I mean, thanks for understanding."

"I'm not sure I do," I said. "But you're welcome."

And in the morning, she offered to let me borrow her iridescent blue dragonfly earrings. "They'd look great with your outfit," she said. (My "outfit" was a blue shirt and black jeans. I don't spend too much time thinking about clothes.)

I guess even just the *idea* of having her own space was cheering Juliet up. Which made things easier for me. So I should have been glad. Except it also still hurt, knowing that getting rid of me was the thing that was making her happy. Ugh! I tried to stop thinking about it. I accepted the earrings, and we made a plan to meet in front of the old red brick school on Route 20 — I mean the Stage Road — after school.

When we arrived at the school nobody else seemed to be around. Yay! Maybe we were the first team this time. It wasn't raining out, but it was chilly, so Emma, Zoe, and I stamped our feet and swung our arms while we waited for Juliet to show up.

The old school was actually a pretty cool building, now that I really *looked* at it. It was three stories high, with tall, arched windows trimmed in white and an impressive row of two-story white pillars across the entrance. A carved stone sign above the door read CLOVERDALE PRIMARY SCHOOL, but in front of the building there was a wooden sign with gold letters on a maroon background that read MCDANIEL RESIDENCE FOR ELDERLY WOMEN.

As I glanced at one of the windows, I saw a face looking out, a face topped with a mass of curly white hair. It must have been one of the residents. She smiled and waved at me, and I smiled and waved back.

"I wonder if Mr. Drudge is waiting," I said, blowing on my hands. My fingers were freezing.

"Hope so," said Zoe. "Since we're totally clueless about where to go in there, or what to do."

"Hey!" It was Juliet, running toward us. "Thanks for waiting, you guys. It's *freezing* out!"

"You didn't tell anybody at school about us figuring out the clue, did you?" I asked.

She made a face. "Come on, Ophelia. Do I *look* like an idiot?"

"No comment," I said, laughing. "Kidding!" I added. "Come on, let's go in." I led the way up the wide granite stairs that brought us to the big doors of the main entrance. We pushed open the doors and walked inside. "Whoa!" I said. "It's steamy in here!" It felt like it was about a hundred degrees. What a difference from outside.

"The residents prefer it that way." Mr. Drudge appeared, stepping out from behind a pillar. He nodded to us. "Welcome! And congratulations on being the first team to arrive."

"Yesss!" Juliet threw a fist into the air.

"Where do we go?" asked Zoe. "Where's the auditorium? What's the task? How can there be horses in a place like this?"

She had a point. The place — at least the reception area — was spotless. Every piece of furniture was gleaming, and the floors were shining. It smelled like lemon furniture polish. Not at all what I thought an old folks' home would smell like.

Mr. Drudge smiled at Zoe's questions. It was a

thin, restrained smile, but he *did* smile. "All will be revealed in time," he said mysteriously. "Now, if you'll just follow me —"

He turned — and almost walked into an old woman who had come up behind him, shuffling along with her metal walker. "Excuse me, ma'am," he said with a stiff little bow.

She ignored him and made a beeline for our little group. "How lovely!" she said. Her wrinkled face was glowing beneath a crown of white hair. It had to be the woman I'd waved to from outside. "Mabel! Eunice! The children have come to sing for us again!"

Two other women appeared from around the corner. "Oh, wonderful!" one of them cried, clapping her hands. "Visitors!"

Juliet and I glanced at each other. "We're not —" Juliet began.

But then another elderly woman, this one so stooped and tiny that everybody but Emma towered over her, came toward us at a surprisingly fast pace, leaning on her cane. "More singers!" she crowed. "It must be *months* since we had any children come to sing. Marvelous! What will you sing for us? Come into the parlor. Come along, don't be shy." She moved off, clearly expecting us to follow her and the others. They'd all turned to go into a room to the left, which had to be the parlor.

I looked at Mr. Drudge. He just raised his eyebrows and smiled that little smile again. Then I looked at my teammates. "What do you think?" I asked.

"It'll make them happy," Emma answered. She looked a little sad herself. I had a feeling she was thinking of her grandmother, who died last spring. She and Emma were very close.

I could tell Juliet was dying to get to that auditorium. So was Zoe. I was eager to get there, too. But would it hurt to sing a song or two? "Let's do it," I said.

And we sang.

Zoe asked if the women had any requests and Annabel — the one with the cane — suggested Christmas carols. It seemed a little early for that, but what the hey? We started with "Silent Night" and moved on through "Deck the Halls" and "The First Noel." Our audience kept growing as more and more women came into the room. Some of them sang along. Others just nodded and smiled at us. It was actually kind of fun. We really got into it. Emma and Zoe and I even tried out some harmonies we've been learning in chorus. We had whipped into "Jingle Bells" and were singing at the top of our lungs when I heard Zoe squeak on a high note. She was staring toward the doorway. I turned to look. Peter Brown, Gary Irish, and two eighth-graders I don't really know were standing there watching us, grinning and whispering to one another.

How totally embarrassing! And annoying. While we were entertaining the Golden Girls, the next team had arrived!

Somehow we made it to the end of the song. Then I gave a little curtsy. "And that's the end of our program," I announced. "Next, the boys of U-28 will entertain you with some of *their* favorite songs!"

Ha. Got them. Peter looked stunned, and he turned as if to run out the door, but the old women started clapping and calling for them to come in. They had no choice. "Don't *really* sing your favorite songs," I whispered to Peter as I passed him on my way out. "I doubt this audience is into rap."

Mr. Drudge was waiting for us. "I know the residents enjoyed that," he said.

"So, where's this auditorium?" Zoe asked him again.

"I'd be delighted to show you there," answered Mr. Drudge. "Follow me." He began to walk along the polished corridor.

Juliet trotted to keep up with him. "What about these 'dusty ancient treasures'?" she asked. "Do they have something to do with the fortune?"

"Everything in the treasure hunt has to do with the fortune," was all Mr. Drudge would say.

Juliet looked frustrated, but she wasn't ready to give up. "Is the fortune a *thing*?" she asked, "Like jewels, or a valuable piece of art?"

Then Zoe joined in. "Or is it money?" she asked. "Piles and wads of hundred-dollar bills?"

You could tell what *she'd* been dreaming about.

Mr. Drudge just shook his head. "All will be revealed in time," he said. "For now, I suggest you concentrate on the matter at hand."

He led us down the hall, pointing out the cafeteria and a crafts room, to a set of big doors at the end. "These doors haven't been opened in some time," he said. "According to the owners of the building, they just don't have the time or money to deal with this room." He turned a key in the lock and pulled the doors open.

"Yikes," breathed Zoe, who was standing next to me.

So this was the auditorium. It was a big room, two stories high, with tall windows that were so dusty they hardly let in any sun. It was positively crepuscular[15] in there. But there was enough light to see that the place was a mess. Jumbled rows of seats, along with piles of boxes and other junk, covered most of the floor. Yes, there were red cur-

---

[15]crepuscular: dim, resembling twilight

tains, but they were dusty and faded and hung crookedly over the stage, which was just a raised platform along one end of the room. The stage was *crammed* with junk, some of it covered with old white sheets.

"I don't see any horses," murmured Juliet.

"You will," promised Mr. Drudge. "Trust me. But there's much to do before you find your *true* task. Now. There's a big moving truck parked outside the back exit. An auctioneer has agreed to take away the contents of this room and sell it off. A share of the proceeds will go toward renovating this room. But first, it has to be cleaned out."

"And *we're* supposed to do it?" Zoe stared at him. "The four of us?"

Thin Drudge smile. "There are professional movers here to do the heavy work. And I expect more help is on the way."

He was right. Before we'd even figured out where to start, Peter and his team arrived. Helena and Viola and their friends were next, and three other teams showed up before the afternoon was over.

We got a lot done that first day. We helped haul old furniture out to the moving truck, got the curtains down (with a little help from the McDaniel maintenance man), and even made a first attempt at washing the windows (ditto — he had a nice tall ladder) so we'd be able to see better when we came back on Thursday.

You know what? It turned out to be fun. We found all kinds of neat stuff, including some funny old textbooks from the twenties and thirties. Mr. Drudge said we could pull out anything we wanted to look through more carefully, so I put some of those aside. We also saved a box full of old pictures.

But we didn't find the horses. Not that day.

After school the next day, a few more kids showed up and the work went even faster. That is, after we all had sung. Stopping to give a short concert in the parlor seemed to be the price of admission to the McDaniel Residence. We worked for a long time and finally cleared out enough stuff so we could make it up onto the stage itself. I was working with Zoe, clearing away a pile of boxes full of old lighting fixtures, when I glanced over and saw Juliet lift the corner of one of the sheets covering a pile of stuff. She froze. Then she gasped.

"Horses!" she yelled.

Everybody came running.

Juliet pulled the sheet away and we all stood staring. She was right. There was a horse underneath that sheet. A cast-iron horse, or at least a horse *head*, with a flowing mane and wild eyes. "Whoa!" said Michelle Wiley. "Check it out!"

"Cool!" said Peter Brown. "But — what are they and what are they doing here? They're, like, statues or something."

Juliet was kneeling near the horse head. "It's hollow," she said, examining it more closely.

It was Helena's turn to gasp. She was sitting cross-legged on the stage, looking through the old box of pictures we'd found. "Check it out!" she said, jumping up to show us a picture.

"Not now," I said. "We're trying to figure out what's going on with these horses."

Helena shoved the picture under my nose, so I couldn't help looking at it.

"Oh, my God!" I said. "The horses!"

"What about them?" asked Juliet, coming over to look.

"They're part of a fountain," I said, passing the picture around. It showed people in old-fashioned clothes, gathered in the green near the gazebo. In the background, a fountain with three rearing horses as its centerpiece sprayed water high into the air. "A fountain that used to be on the green, near the gazebo," I finished. Suddenly, I remembered interrupting Mrs. Sparrow the other day, just as she was saying something about a fountain on the green. I didn't know what she was talking about at the time; there's never been a fountain on the green since I lived in Cloverdale. And I was too impatient to ask about it then. But now it came back to me. I told the others. "You know that big patch of overgrown weeds near the clump of trees? That must be where it was."

"'You'll find the third clue on the day that sleeping horses spout and spray!'" Peter recited. "Yes! That's it! Fountains spout and spray!"

We all went over to pull the rest of the sheets off and stare down at the horses.

"They're beautiful!" I said. "But what are they doing in here?"

"I can answer that." Mr. Drudge stepped out from the wings. He was always appearing out of nowhere! "Years ago, there was a bad drought," he explained. "The townspeople decided the fountain was a waste of water, so it was dismantled."

"But why is it *here*?" I asked.

"I think I know," said Juliet, who was rummaging around in the pile of fountain parts. She lifted out a brass plaque and held it up. "'Donated by the class of 1911,'" she read. "'In memory of our dear classmate Wilma Grover.'"

"She must have been one of Grandpa Grover's relatives!" I said. "And her classmates at this school donated the fountain."

Mr. Drudge nodded. "That's one reason it was so important to him to bring the fountain back to life," he said. "And now that you've found it, your task has begun."

"Begun!" Peter Brown cried. "After all that work?"

"Remember the clue," Mr. Drudge said. "Think about your task."

The next afternoon, we were all on hand again. And I'd called Olivia, thinking she might like to take some pictures of the fountain, if we got it running.

A bunch of us had met at school at lunchtime to figure it out, and we'd come up with a plan. We would haul all the fountain pieces outside, onto the grounds of the McDaniel Residence. We'd pile the pieces together, as best we could. And then we'd run a garden hose to it, to see if it still worked.

It *had* to, if we were going to get the next clue.

It may sound unbelievable, but we made it happen. Us! A bunch of kids. We worked all afternoon, hauling those huge pieces of cast iron and putting them together like a 3-D puzzle. I'd brought a roll of duct tape, which Vermonters use to fix just about everything from cars to torn ski jackets, and Gary Irish and I managed to connect one end of the hose to what looked like the main water supply pipe for the fountain. Finally, just as the sun was about to go down, we gathered outside, zipping up our jackets and stamping our feet to stay warm. Juliet, who stood by the hose faucet, called out, "Ready?"

"Ready!" we chorused. The residents were watching from the windows. Mr. Drudge stood nearby, wearing a black wool overcoat, a black bowler, and his usual barely-there smile. I was holding my breath. Juliet turned on the water. There was a pause. Then, a second later, water started to spray out of the mouths of all three horses.

We all cheered and jumped around, hugging one another. Olivia shot picture after picture, and her friend Janie took notes on a pad. Olivia said Janie was a reporter, and they were hoping to sell the story to the paper if it came out well.

"Hey, what's that?" Katherine and her team had showed up just in time. Now Pete Pelkey was stepping forward to pick something up. "This came out of one of the horse's mouths," he said, holding up a small clear plastic tube. He pulled it apart, and a little piece of paper fluttered out. Katherine grabbed it.

"It's the next clue," she said.

Chapter Fourteen

She read it out loud. Then Mr. Drudge stepped forward to hand out copies to everyone.

A good Stillson wrench and a cow on a flag,
Flypaper, yeast, and a brown paper bag,
Seeds for a garden and a brush for your pet,
An apron, some humbugs, a badminton set,

A needle and thread and a ribbon of pink,
A kerosene lantern, some tiddlywinks,
A potbellied stove and some licorice, too,
Find all these things to complete your next clue.

"Excellent," murmured Zoe next to me. "It's a scavenger hunt. I'm *great* at these. Once, in third grade at my old school? My best friend had a scavenger hunt for her birthday party. My team won by a *mile*."

I read the clue over again quickly. "It doesn't look too hard," I said. "How about if we meet tomorrow afternoon at my house?" I knew everybody had chores and family stuff to do on Saturday mornings. "We can round up a few of these things," I pointed to the poem, "then have our sleepover and finish the rest up on Sunday morning." I'd invited my friends over to help me move into my new room and then spend the night.

"Sounds like a plan," said Emma.

"I'm there," agreed Zoe.

We stepped back to take one last look at the fountain. Even though we'd just barely stuck it together, it looked awesome. Then I turned off the hose, and Peter coiled it up and put it away.

To: DParker
From: WrrdGrrl
Re: Treasure
Wait until you see the fountain we discovered! It's so beautiful. I can almost picture how it would look in the middle of the green. Maybe someday . . .
The next clue looks pretty easy compared to the last one. Wish me luck!
Moving into the tiny room tomorrow. I'll let you know how it is.
Luv you — O.

Chapter Fifteen

"Check it out!" Helena was waving something at me.

"What? Put that down," I said, swatting it away. It was Saturday morning, and I wasn't totally awake yet. I was still in my robe and my fuzzy leopard-print slippers, and I was poking through the kitchen cupboards to see if we had any Cream of Wheat. I'm the only one who can stand it, besides Poppy, so it's usually way in the back of the shelf.

"It's *us*!" she said. "In the paper!"

"The paper? Us? What are you talking about?" I spotted the familiar label. "Ah, there it is," I said, reaching for the box. Then I turned to look at Helena. She was holding up that morning's newspaper so I could see the picture on the front page.

"Hey, cool!" I said. There we were, a whole bunch of us, standing around the fountain outside the McDaniel Residence. Water was spouting out of the horses' mouths. I put down the Cream of Wheat and sat down at the table to take a better look. "Oh, man!" I said. "Look who's right in front!" I stared at Katherine's smiling face.

"I know," said Helena. "Can you believe it? Her team didn't even do any of the work!"

Typical. Still, it was great to see the picture in the paper. I could see myself and Juliet and Zoe, but Emma must have been behind some other kids. She wouldn't mind, since she hates pictures of herself anyway. There was Olivia's name, in tiny type just under the right-hand corner. And beneath the picture were a few paragraphs about the treasure hunt and how it had led us to the fountain. "Town Treasure Hunt Yields Splashy Prize" was the headline, and beneath that it said "by Janie O'Hare."

The phone rang just then, and I grabbed it. It was Olivia. "Did you see it?" she asked. "Isn't it cool? My first published picture!" I could hardly hear her talking because someone else was making a racket at her end.

"It's the coolest," I agreed. "Who's that screaming in the background?"

"That's Janie," Olivia said. "It's her first published article. She's psyched."

Everybody was psyched. (Well, except Mom. I'd describe her as proud as punch, instead.) The phone kept ringing all morning, which made it hard to get to the chores I was supposed to do: clean the laundry room, vacuum the living room, and scrub the bathtub. I had also planned to clean out the junk room, but it was too much of a mess in there. I peeked in, but I shut the door fast. There were bags of old clothes waiting to be sorted or mended, old curtains that Mom was planning to make into a quilt someday, a baby stroller (why were we saving *that*?), boxes of pictures waiting to go into albums, and a whole pile of shoes nobody was wearing anymore. No way was I going to deal with that on my own! Juliet was going to have to help, and maybe Emma and Zoe would, too.

I read through the clue once, and even managed to track down one item on the list: the brush we use to groom Bob (when we remember). It was all chewed up and full of dog hair, but I figured that just made it more authentic.

Zoe and Emma did a little better. Zoe arrived first, waving a badminton racquet as I let her in. "I've got the whole set," she said proudly. "It was in our attic. And I found some old lettuce seeds in the garage. Do you think they'll do?" She dug through her backpack, then held up a tattered envelope with a picture of iceberg lettuce on it.

I shrugged. "I don't see why not," I told her.

Emma had actually stopped by Mrs. Sparrow's house to borrow an apron, and Mrs. Sparrow had given her a packet of yeast along with it.

And Juliet, who'd also been busy with chores that morning, had rummaged around behind the fridge for a brown paper bag from the supermarket.

We spread everything out on the (beautifully vacuumed!) living room floor.

"So, that's six items already!" I said, ticking them off on my fingers. "This shouldn't take long at all."

Just then, Katherine turned up, leaning against the arched doorway. "Good luck moving a potbellied stove by yourselves," she said. "Even my guys had a little trouble with that one."

I stared at her. "Your team already found a potbellied stove?" I asked. That couldn't have been easy. Lots of people heat their houses with woodstoves around here, but most of them are modern ones, glossy blue or red, with glass windows so you can see the fire. I've seen pictures of shiny black potbellied stoves, but I don't think I've ever seen a real one. I'd been thinking we'd have to go to an antiques store or something. And even then, I wasn't thinking we'd actually try to *move* the thing. I thought we'd take a picture or something. Doesn't that count, in most scavenger hunts?

Katherine just gave me a smug little smile, turned, and disappeared.

That was it. It was time to get her back for sending us on that wild-goose chase in the rain. "She's asking for it," I said. "Isn't she?"

Emma shrugged. "I don't know," she said carefully. "She doesn't bother *me* that much. But I can see how she'd get to you."

"I'm in," said Zoe. "It'll be fun. Where should we send her? I vote for the town dump."

"Ooh," Juliet said. "Nasty." We go to the dump with Poppy on the first Saturday of every month, to drop off our trash and recycling. It's not the *prettiest* place in Cloverdale, or the sweetest-smelling.

"I have a better idea," Emma said slowly.

We all turned to look at her. Emma smiled. "I know you think I'm not good at being mean," she said, "but listen to this. I stopped by the firehouse on the way here to ask if I could borrow their Vermont flag. You know, because it has a cow on it?"

Wow. I hadn't even started to figure out that part of the clue. But now that she mentioned it, I could picture our state flag. It shows a tree, some haystacks, and this big old cow, all on a blue background. I think it's our state seal or something. Of course!

"So where is it?" I asked.

"They said no way! They've had about fifteen kids asking for it, and it's driving the chief crazy."

"So?" I asked. "How does that help us?"

"Easy," said Emma devilishly. "We let Katherine overhear us talking about how they're giving out free Vermont flags at the firehouse. You know, little ones. She and her team will go over there acting like they expect something, and the chief will totally lose it!"

We all know Chief Johnson. He's not the friendly-pal-to-kids type of fireman, like on *Sesame Street*. He's an old grouch who comes to the elementary school every year to yell at kids about fire prevention.

My mouth fell open. I always knew Emma was smart, but I never guessed she had it in her to be an Evil Mastermind. "Awesome," I said. It wasn't quite as bad as making us ride all over town on a cold, rainy day, but it would still feel great to get Katherine back.

And so the deed was done. It wasn't hard to make sure that Katherine overheard us talking about the free flags down at the firehouse. It was a total kick to see her blast right out of the house to claim one for herself. And it was incredibly satisfying to see her come slinking back, still red-faced. I could hardly wait until word got around school.

Meanwhile, Emma and Zoe and Juliet helped me move all of the junk out of the junk room. Mostly we just piled it into the upstairs part of our barn, which I'll probably pay for when Poppy gets back home; he hates when we shove stuff into his neatly organized space. It was the easiest place to put everything, since the barn is connected to the house, and the door between the two is right next to my new room. Then we swept out the room and mopped the floor. We moved in my bed and chair and a small night table and a reading lamp. I took the bulletin board, too; since I wouldn't have any windows to look out of I figured I'd put up a bunch of outdoor pictures. When I'd made my bed with clean sheets and tucked Doogey into my blue quilt, I stepped back to take a look around.

"It's not bad," I said. "A little . . . cozy, but not bad at all!"

"I love it," Emma told me. "A little room, all your own. It's perfect!"

"Except for one thing," I said. "We can't all fit in here for our sleepover." It was true. The room is so tiny that there wasn't even space on the floor for two sleeping bags. That's why we ended up camped out in the living room, which is where we usually spend most of our sleepovers anyway, watching videos and eating popcorn.

It was funny. After all that stuff about needing her personal space, Juliet ended up sleeping on the living room couch, sharing it with Zoe. Emma passed out curled up on the love seat. And me? I ended up slipping off to my new room, after everyone else had fallen asleep. Suddenly, I couldn't wait to see what it felt like to be in my own little place. Know what? It felt good. Jenny-cat thought so, too. She followed me into the room and slept curled up by my side, a warm, content little bundle of good company.

When I woke up, I headed straight for the study to report to Poppy.

To: DParker
From: WrrdGrrl
Subject: Personal space
I slept in my new room last night! No snoring. Nobody's light on when I'm ready to sleep. Just me, Jenny, and Doogey and four walls of my own. Maybe I could learn to like this. . . .

Chapter Sixteen

I signed off and headed downstairs to see if my friends were awake yet. It was late by then, but Zoe and Juliet were still totally out of it. Emma was sitting up, stretching and yawning. Nearby, Charles did cat stretches and kitty-yawns. He must have slept on the love seat with her.

"I had the weirdest dream," Emma said, rubbing her eyes, "all about a potbellied stove, only it was, like, animated. It was running around, chasing after me."

"Hmm," I said, stroking my chin. "Sounds like you have some deep psychological feelings about potbellied stoves."

"Who? What?" asked Juliet, waking up. "Where's the stove? Have you guys been out scavenging without me?"

That woke Zoe up, too. "What's going on?" she asked, pushing her hair out of her face as she sat up.

"Nothing," I said, laughing. "We're just discussing our dreams."

"Oh." She lay back again. Zoe is not exactly a morning person. "So can I go back to sleep?"

"No way!" I grabbed her pillow. "Time to get up. We have a clue to solve." I bopped her with the pillow. You know, just to get her moving.

She grabbed Juliet's pillow and bopped me back, and then Emma got into it, bopping Juliet for no real reason. Soon we were in the midst of a full-scale pillow fight, yelling and giggling and jumping around, slamming one another with the pillows until the feathers were flying. That's why I love my friends: They have no problem acting like seven-year-olds.

"Whoa, okay! Time!" I said, holding up my hands in a T. Feathers drifted down around me as I collapsed onto the couch between Zoe and Juliet. Zoe bopped me once more.

"That makes us even," she said. "Since you started it."

"What's for breakfast?" Juliet asked. "I'm starving."

"I don't know, "I said. "Let's go see what everybody else is having." But the kitchen was empty. There were a few dishes in the sink, but no sign of the twins or Katherine. Or Mom, for that matter. She was probably already out doing errands. I opened the fridge and peered inside.

"Here's a note," said Emma, who was sitting at the table. "It says, 'Good monkey! Twins told me about the sprank. See you thence! XO, Mom.'"

"Sprank?" asked Juliet. "What's a sprank?"

"That's what it looks like." Emma giggled. "Her writing is even worse than *my* mom's."

Juliet leaned over her shoulder. "Store," she said. "It says 'store.' And that's good morning, not good *monkey*, and it's not *thence*, it's there. See you there." We're all pretty good at deciphering Mom's griffonage[16].

"Good *thing* they went to the store," I grumbled, with my head still stuck in the fridge. "There's no yogurt, no orange juice, and only enough milk for one bowl of cereal."

Juliet rummaged around in the cupboards. "We have some stale English muffins," she reported.

"Works for me," said Zoe.

Emma was still looking over the note. "I don't get this," she said. "What does she mean about seeing you at the store? Are you supposed to meet her down at Price Chopper?"

"I don't think so." I grabbed the butter and a jar of blueberry jam and set them on the table. "She didn't say anything about that last night. And we never go out there except *with* her. It's too far to walk or carry groceries."

"So, why would she say that?" asked Emma. "And what store does she mean?"

---

[16]griffonage: sloppy handwriting

"I don't know," I said a little impatiently. "It's just a note, Emma."

"Something seems weird about it," she said.

"Something seems weird about this morning," Juliet agreed. "The house is so quiet. I'm going to go see if Katherine's still sleeping." She ran upstairs and came back fast. "She's not!" she said. "She's gone, too."

I popped a couple of English muffins into the toaster. "So?" I said. But I was starting to wonder myself. Then the phone rang.

Juliet answered it. "Hello?" She listened, then turned to us. "It's Olivia, on her cell phone. She wants to know why we're not down at the store."

"*What* store?" I asked.

Juliet listened again. "She says to look out the window. Toward the green."

We ran to the front of the house to look out the window. "What's going *on*?" I asked. Across the green from our house, over on East Street, there was all kinds of activity. People were milling around, and there was a bunch of cars parked along the road.

It was too far to be able to identify individual faces, but I was betting that the person waving her arms frantically was Olivia. She was yelling so loud over her cell phone that even I could hear her, and Juliet was holding the phone away from her ear.

"Olivia says we should just get over there," Juliet reported. "It has to do with the treasure hunt."

Oops. Our team had blown it. Maybe we'd been too casual about solving this clue. Maybe we'd spent too much time and energy on fooling Katherine. Maybe we'd wasted our morning having pillow fights. Whatever. It was time to get on the case. "Let's go!" I said, grabbing my jacket from the hall closet. I suddenly realized what store my mom must have meant.

We ran across the green and arrived, panting, in front of the general store that's been there all my life. Most of the time it's either been closed, with the windows boarded over and no lights on, or open but not really interesting enough to go into.

Something had changed.

There was a banner across the front of the store. WELCOME, TREASURE HUNTERS, it read in big red letters on a white background. GRAND RE-OPENING. There were little knots of people hanging around talking excitedly, and little kids were running in and out of the store.

Olivia ran over to meet us, a camera hanging from her neck and another in her hand. "Isn't this cool?" she asked. "This is all because of my picture and Janie's article. Well, I mean, it's because of the treasure hunt, too. Isn't this cool?" she asked again.

I was still trying to figure out how it all fit together. Then I saw Helena and Viola coming out the door. Helena was sucking on a red lollipop, and Viola had a purple one. "Hey, you finally made it!" said Helena. "It's about time. Even Katherine and her team are here already."

"What's going on?" I asked.

Viola smiled. "Go inside and see for yourself," she told me.

I glanced around at Emma, Zoe, and Juliet, who all looked as bewildered as I felt. "Let's go," I said, shrugging.

The store was packed with people. But the first one I spotted was the ever-soigné[17] Mr. Drudge. Dressed as usual in his dark suit and tie, he loomed over the crowd of little kids surging around him. "Welcome!" he said when he saw us. "And congratulations on solving the clue."

"Solving the clue?" I asked. "We didn't —"

Emma nudged me. "Check it out," she said, nodding toward a gleaming black potbellied stove in the middle of the main aisle. No wonder the

[17]soigné: elegant, neatly groomed

118

store was so warm and cozy! Next to the stove there was a table set up with coffee, cider, and doughnuts, with a sign reading HELP YOURSELF. I looked around the store and saw tidy, well-organized shelves packed with all kinds of stuff: everything you could want. There was a rack of flower and vegetable seeds, a hardware section with wrenches hanging in orderly rows on the wall, a sewing corner stocked with every color of thread and ribbons, a display of flags, and a pet section featuring bowls, brushes, leashes, toys, and treats.

There was a sandwich counter at one end of the shop, where a girl was scrambling to fix orders for all the hungry people who were lined up waiting. I even spotted an old-fashioned soda fountain along the back wall, with stools and a counter.

I nodded. Duh. "I get it," I said. "It wasn't a scavenger hunt at all. Everything on that list is in one place. Here."

"That's it!" Mr. Drudge nodded. "Cloverdale has a real general store again, thanks to these folks." He gestured toward two people standing near him, a man and a woman, both shorter than me, with dark hair and eyes. Two small children clung to the woman's legs, peeking at us shyly from behind her skirt. "May I introduce the Nguyens?" he said.

"Pleased to meet you," said the man, with a little bow, after we'd told them our names. "And this is Mai, and her brother, Tam." The children looked up at us with shy smiles, and we grinned back. They were adorable!

I was still totally confused. "But —" I began. "How — why — ?"

Mrs. Nguyen smiled gently. "Mr. Grover was our sponsor," she said in a soft voice. "He helped us come here from Vietnam, where we were shop-keepers. He left us some money to fix up this store. And now he has brought all of you here as well." She gestured around at the happy crowd. "So now the town will know we are here."

"And the town couldn't be happier about it," put in Mom, who had just come up behind me. "This is exactly what Cloverdale needed. A place to buy whatever you might need, without having to get in your car and go to that huge, ugly super-market. Milk, some bread or eggs, some shoe pol-ish —"

"A needle and thread and a ribbon of pink," I added.

"And some humbugs, whatever they are," put in Zoe.

"Speaking of which," said Mr. Drudge, "are you ready for your task?"

"What is it this time?" asked Juliet.

"This time," said Mr. Drudge, "your task is entirely simple, and very pleasurable." He pulled a roll of pennies out of his pocket and gave us each a few. They were brand-new and extremely shiny. "Your task is to spend these here. And be certain to keep your receipt!"

I looked down at the three cents in my hand. "Um, thanks," I said, trying to sound grateful. I mean, what can you buy for three cents?

Mr. Drudge just smiled his thin little smile. "Enjoy yourselves!" he said, and waved us on our way.

We smiled and nodded again at the Nguyens, and I waved at the kids, who jumped back behind their mom, shrieking with giggles. Then we started to explore the store. It didn't take us long to figure out where to spend our pennies: Lined up along a low counter near the front door were rows and rows of jars full of penny candy. (We'd probably missed it when we came in because there were so many kids in front of it!) There were peppermint sticks and gummy bears, rock candy and chocolate drops and sour balls, long scrolls of paper covered with candy buttons, and at least four kinds of licorice.

And there was a jar full of humbugs, which turned out to be red-and-white-striped mint candies. I had to have one of those. I also chose a peach-flavored lollipop and one chocolate kiss.

"This is great," I said, handing my three cents to the smiling woman behind the counter, who must have been related to the Nguyens.

"Don't forget to keep your receipt," she reminded me, handing over a small bag.

Juliet picked out some rock candy, a piece of saltwater taffy, and a sour ball.

Emma went for three pieces of black licorice; it's her favorite.

And Zoe got a red-hot jawbreaker, a humbug, and a lemon lollipop.

I felt like a little kid again, getting excited over candy. But when was candy ever that fun? Even Miranda got into it, spending her own pennies after she'd pulled up in her squad car. By then, we were hanging out outside the store, just checking out the action. It seemed as if everybody in town came to the store that day. Every team of kids showed up, plus their little brothers and sisters. People's parents came, too. You may think it's pathetic, but this store was a big deal for Cloverdale.

We all hung out for a long time, eating our candy and watching people come and go. Olivia snapped tons of pictures, and Janie was scribbling notes for another article. Then, finally, Mr. Drudge stepped out onto the store's porch. "May I have your attention, please?" he asked.

Chapter Seventeen

It didn't take long for the crowd to quiet down. There's something about Mr. Drudge: He makes you want to be polite. Oh, and also, we all wanted to hear the next clue!

"It's time to announce the final clue for this treasure hunt. Did you all save your receipts?"

I felt for mine. I'd stuck it into the back pocket of my jeans, and at first I couldn't find it. But after a moment of panic, I pulled it out. "Yes," I chorused, along with everyone else.

"Each one has a series of numbers on it," Mr. Drudge went on.

I looked down at my receipt and nodded. True enough.

"Those numbers are your clue."

"What?" I heard Emma murmur next to me. She was staring at her receipt, frowning. She wasn't the only one.

Mr. Drudge didn't give us much time to think about the clue. He ignored our bewildered looks and kept on talking. "And this time, you'll get your task at the same time. Your final task is to look on your shelves at home and find a book that you once loved very much. Bring that book to the library on Tuesday at three-thirty."

There was a brief silence.

"Why?" Billy Smallwood asked the question on everyone's mind.

"Why?" asked Mr. Drudge. "Because the library needs books, especially books for younger children. And each of you must have at least one that you can donate, so everyone in town can grow up reading good books. It's a simple thing, and something Mr. Grover thought was very, very important." He gave us a slight smile and nodded briskly. "That's all, then," he said. "'Til Tuesday. Or until someone solves the last clue, whichever comes first." He walked down the stairs, opened the back door of a black car that was waiting at the curb, and got in. The car drove off, leaving us all staring.

Chapter Eighteen

There were a few moments of silence as the car turned the corner and disappeared down Route 20. Then everybody started to talk at once. Emma, Zoe, Juliet, and I clustered together, looking down at the receipts in our hands and comparing to make sure they were the same. They were. All four were equally confusing. Just a list of numbers, nothing else. Like this:

24/1
1999
14:50
974.317
112–113

I groaned. I can handle words. But numbers? Not really my thing. Emma's good at math, but it's always been a struggle for me. It took me forever to learn my times tables, and I still sometimes have trouble with division. Fractions? Forget it.

"What do you think?" I asked Emma. "Is it some kind of algebra problem or something?"

She shook her head slowly. "I have no idea what this could mean," she said.

All around us, teams were puzzling over the clue. Well, except Katherine's team. She was standing there looking annoyed, while her teammates argued.

"Give it to me," Ryan said, grabbing the receipt out of Pete's hands.

"Hey!" yelled Pete. "Give that back! You got one of your own."

"I lost it," Ryan said, turning his shoulder and holding the receipt high up so Pete, who's pretty short, couldn't reach it.

"Is that my fault?" Pete asked. "Come on, dude, give it to me. You just know I'm going to solve it first. That's why you stole it."

"No way could you solve that!" put in Billy Smallwood. "Not a chance." He held up his receipt. "Now I, on the other hand, already know what three of these numbers stand for."

I could tell he was bluffing.

Pete and Ryan could, too. Both of them burst out laughing. "Sure, Brainiac," said Pete. "You'll solve this one just like you solved all the others. Not."

"We'll see," said Billy.

They were so into their argument that they didn't even notice right away when Katherine walked off by herself, leaving them to it.

Juliet and I exchanged a look and a shrug. At least Katherine's team wouldn't be a threat. That much was obvious. On the other hand, I wasn't sure our team would do all that well, either. This clue seemed way harder than the others, and the others weren't exactly easy. My team spent some time that afternoon looking over the numbers and trying things like adding them up in different ways (Emma's idea), or trying to figure out if they stood for letters of the alphabet (Zoe's idea). Nothing seemed to work, and finally we gave up, figuring we'd try again the next day.

Later that night, I was practicing my flute. I'm working on a Mozart piece that has a really hard run of notes in one section. I'd tried all the tricks my flute teacher, Mira, has taught me. I broke down the run into individual notes. I played it slowly, then gradually speeded it up. I tried different fingerings. Nothing was working. I was totally frustrated. Also, my flute sounded so loud in that tiny room that it was giving me a headache. Jenny had meowed to be let out before I even finished playing my warm-up scales. I tried the run one more time and missed the F sharp *again*. Argh!

Suddenly, there was a loud pounding at my door.

"Who's there?" I asked.

"It's me."

Katherine's voice.

"Hello, me," I said, opening the door. "Why were you pounding so hard?"

"I wasn't at first," Katherine said. "I started off with a polite little tap. But you were screeching away on that thing" — she pointed to the flute I was still holding — "and you couldn't hear me."

"Excuse me? *Screeching*? I know I didn't have the notes right, but I was hardly *screeching*." I've been working hard on my embouchure[18], and Mira says my tone is really coming along.

"Oh, you know what I mean," she said. "Anyway, let me in."

I raised my eyebrows. Katherine doesn't often come calling. That fact alone made me curious enough to step aside so she could walk into my room.

She looked around. It only took a second. "Nice" she said, nodding. "How long is your sentence?"

"Ha-ha," I said. "This may look like a prison cell to you, but it's freedom to me. Freedom to do whatever I want, whenever I want." At the moment I couldn't think of a single thing that I actually wanted to do, but it sounded good.

---

[18]embouchure: the shape you make with your mouth when you play a wind instrument

"Sure. Whatever." Katherine plopped herself down on the bed and started plucking at one of the purple threads in my quilt.

"What's up?" I asked, taking my flute apart and putting it into its case. I figured I was done with practice for the night.

"Something has to be up?" she fired back. "What if I just came by to hang out, do the sister thing?"

"Right," I said. "The sister thing. So what's up?" Katherine doesn't do much of anything without a reason. And she's not big on hanging out just to chat.

She plucked some more.

"Hey, don't pull my quilt apart," I said.

She looked down at her hand as if she'd just realized what it was doing. "Oh. Sorry." She shook her head. "Look, this is hard for me."

"*What* is?" I asked. Her presence in my room was still a complete mystery to me.

"Asking for a favor. Admitting I messed up. Coming to you for help."

Whoa. Katherine? Coming to *me* for help? This had to be a first.

She was staring down at the quilt. "How did you mess up?" I asked. "And what's the favor?"

Katherine sighed. "I messed up choosing my team, all right? You saw how they are. It's not a team at all. They're all just trying to beat *one another*, to impress me. It's ridiculous. *Your* team works together. Mine's off in a million different directions. We haven't been first to get a clue *once*. We haven't even been close. And now it's the final clue, and whoever gets it will find the fortune and be incredibly rich and happy, and there's no way. Just no way."

She sounded totally frustrated. "But what can I do?" I asked.

She looked at me. "Let me be on your team," she said.

My mouth dropped open. "But —"

She held up a hand. "I know, it's supposed to be teams of four. I won't even claim part of the prize if we win. I just want to have a *chance*."

"What about *your* team?" I asked. "What about the boys?"

She laughed and lay back on my bed. "Forget them. I already told them it was over. They're on their own, which means they *might* solve the clue by New Year's." She picked up Doogey. "Who needs those dumb old boys, right, Doogey?" she asked, putting her nose up against his. Then she sat up and met my eyes. "Please, Ophelia?" she asked quietly.

How could I resist? "We'd have to ask Juliet," I said. "And Emma and Zoe."

"Of course," Katherine said quickly. I saw a little smile on her face. She knew she was going to get her way, once again.

Or was it that? "Wait a minute," I said. "Is this some kind of a trick? Are you pretending to join our team just so you can sabotage[19] us?"

She lost the smile. "No, no!" she said. "Really, Ophelia. I'm totally serious. And we're even now, right? I got you, you got me. That's all over."

"Well, maybe," I said. "But we didn't really get you as bad as you got us."

"You didn't hear Chief Johnson yell at me," she said with a grin. "He's a cranky old guy, that chief."

It was hard to trust Katherine, but somehow I did. I knew it had taken a lot of guts for her to ask me. For that reason alone, I was willing to let her join our team — *if* the others agreed. Well, maybe there was another reason, too. This last clue was a tough one, and I knew we could use all the help we could get. There are a lot of things I could say about Katherine, but I'll never accuse her of lacking brainpower.

[19]sabotage: treacherous secret action, intended to disrupt or ruin something

Chapter Nineteen

"Juliet? It's me." I tapped on the door. How strange was that, to be knocking on the door of what used to be my room!

"Come on in!"

I pushed open the door. Juliet was sitting cross-legged on her bed, a calculator in one hand and her math book spread across her lap. She likes to do her homework that way, instead of at her desk. "What's up?"

I looked around the room. Juliet had spread out a little. She'd moved her bed and chair more toward the middle of the room and had put up a couple of posters on what used to be my side of the room: one of Albert Einstein and one of Venus Williams. She'd shoved my bookcase and desk into the corner. "It looks — *nice* in here," I said. I felt a little like a ghost, like I'd died but had come back to see how the people I'd left behind were acting. Juliet was acting as if I'd never existed.

"Thanks." Juliet closed her math book and put it aside.

I looked longingly at the windows. Even with nothing but dreary November to look at, the windows made a big difference in the room. There's a streetlight opposite our house, and I always liked having that glow come through our windows. It was like having a night-light, not that I'm exactly scared of the dark or anything.

I took a deep breath. The room even *smelled* different already, if that doesn't sound too weird. It didn't have a good or a bad smell before, just a certain smell that was made up of me and Juliet combined. Not, like, our dirty socks or anything. Just our *essence*. My new room didn't really smell like anything except the stuff I'd put in the water when I mopped the floor.

"Ophelia?" Juliet asked. She was staring at me.

"Oh," I said. I'd almost forgotten why I came in the first place. Katherine and I had agreed that it would be better if I approached Juliet. Juliet can be stubborn. You have to know how to handle her, and I do. Or, at least, I did. Things have changed lately. "Oh, right. So, I just had a talk with Katherine."

"A talk?" she asked. "About what?"

"Well," I said slowly, "the thing is, she wants to be on our team."

Juliet hooted. "Ha!" She fell back on her bed. "You told her no way, right?"

"Well," I said again. "Not exactly." I told Juliet the deal. That Katherine would help us work on the clue, but that she wouldn't get any of the prize if we won. "She could be an asset," I finished.

Juliet rolled over onto her stomach, facing away from me. "But we have a great team, just the way it is," she said into her quilt. "We don't *need* anybody else."

I was glad she thought so. "True," I said carefully. "But it couldn't hurt. Katherine might come up with some good ideas. You know, new blood and all that."

"I'm just not sure I trust her." Juliet sat up again. "Do you?"

"Honestly?" I asked. "Yes. About this, anyway. Not about anything else, necessarily. I mean, she's still Katherine."

Juliet giggled. "Okay," she said after a moment. "It's okay with me, if Emma and Zoe agree. Did you ask them yet?"

I shook my head. "It's after nine." The rule in our house is, no making or taking phone calls after nine on a school night. That can be embarrassing if somebody calls here at quarter after. Mom and Poppy are always polite, but firm. "I'll check with them tomorrow."

"Have you looked at the clue any more?" Juliet asked.

"No time," I said. "Anyway, I have no ideas. Do you?"

"Nope. But we'll think of something. What do you think the prize is going to be?"

We talked for a while more. I was surprised that Juliet was so chatty; after all, she was the one who wouldn't talk to me when we were sharing a room. But now it seemed like she didn't want me to leave. Every time I started to say something about finishing my homework, or getting ready for bed, she'd bring up another topic or ask me to look at her math homework. It was weird. But I liked it. It was like old times, before she decided she couldn't stand living with me. I stayed in her room until Mom finally knocked on the door and told us it was time to get to bed.

I stopped in the study to e-mail Poppy about the final clue and the news about Katherine. When I went back to my room afterward, it felt — I don't know. Quiet. Kind of lonely. Small.

I wasn't that interested in the book I had on my night table, but since all my other books were still in my old room I didn't have a choice. I read for a while, but turned out the light much earlier than usual. The room seemed so dark, with no windows and no streetlight.

I didn't sleep too well that night. Maybe I'm actually so used to Juliet's snoring that I miss it when I don't hear it. Still, I knew it was probably good that we were trying this separation thing. Wasn't it?

The next day was a busy one. Mondays always are. During homeroom, I managed to talk to Zoe long enough to tell her that Katherine wanted to be on our team. At first she was shocked. "Queen Katherine is going to lower herself and mix with the commoners?" she asked. "Sorry. That was mean. But what's the deal?"

I went through the whole explanation again, glancing at Mr. Mires now and then. Some mornings he lets us socialize while he takes attendance; others, he expects us to be quiet and listen to the announcements. Fortunately, this seemed to be a socializing day. He was talking to some of the boys about football, and he didn't seem to mind Zoe and me chatting.

"What does Juliet think?" Zoe asked.

"She's fine with it, if you are," I said.

Zoe twirled her pencil. "Okay," she said finally. "Whatever. She just better not try any tricks. And she doesn't get any of the treasure. Right?"

"Right," I said, hoping I wasn't making a big mistake, trusting my sister.

I barely saw Emma all day, because she had an orthodontist appointment at lunchtime. She's always a little crabby after she gets her braces tightened. I can't blame her. It must hurt like crazy. I feel really, really lucky that I probably won't have to get any.

She came late to math, but I'd saved her a seat

next to me. We were supposed to be working on some problems from chapter three in our book, since we had a substitute. The sub did not seem the least bit interested in teaching us anything; she just wanted us to be quiet. I think she was reading a mystery up at Mr. Rosenfeld's desk. Every now and then she'd look up and say something snippy like, "People, let's keep our minds on our work," or "I don't want to hear voices!"

I slipped Emma a note. *How are your teeth? :-(*

Ouch, she wrote back. *I hate Dr. Sturgis.*

What color rubber bands did you get this time? I wrote.

She looked at me and grimaced.

"Yikes!" I said out loud. The sub gave me a look. "Sorry!" I whispered. When she went back to her book, I scribbled a quick note. *Oops! I like them. I just wasn't expecting purple and neon pink.* Then I grabbed the paper back and wrote some more. *Katherine wants to join our team. Tired of the boys. Wants a chance to win. Won't take any of the prize. What do you think?* I'd learned to give the short version by then.

Fine with me, Emma wrote back. *We're not getting anywhere with this clue. Maybe she'll help.* Emma is so easygoing.

After math, I was at my locker getting my social studies book when Katherine passed by. "So?" she asked, tossing her hair as if she didn't care. "What did they say?"

"You're in," I said, closing my locker. "But remember —"

"No prize. I know." She tossed her hair again. "Cool. When do we get together?"

"Not today," I said. "Emma has dance after school, I have flute, plus I'm baby-sitting after. Zoe has basketball practice, and I think Juliet and Mom are going to Burlington. Tomorrow, I guess." We just had to hope that all the other teams were as busy — and as clueless — as we were.

After school, I took the bus that goes out toward my flute teacher's house. Mira lives in this really cool old farmhouse in the middle of nowhere; I love going there. She'd asked me to baby-sit after my lesson this week, so she could give two more lessons. Baby-sitting is not my favorite activity, but Mira's kids are great. Nicholas is five and Hannah is two, and they're both happy, fun kids. I watch them in the playroom while Mira teaches in the music room. We always have a blast, and that afternoon was no exception. I was feeling great because I'd gotten that run in the Mozart piece just right when I played it for Mira. I chased the kids around, playing tickle-monster so they could shriek and run and hide and then jump all over me and tickle me back.

By the time Mom and Juliet stopped by to pick me up, I was exhausted. So I was happy when Mom, who had picked up take-out Chinese food in Burlington, declared that night's dinner a "reading dinner." We have those fairly often when one of our parents is away. Instead of the usual rule where we each have to tell something about our day, the rule is that we each bring something to read to the table. We have a peaceful, quiet dinner, each of us in our own little world. I was looking through a book called *The Quintessential Dictionary*. Poppy gave it to me to celebrate the fact that I came up with the name for our school's literary magazine, *Quintessence*. I've found some excellent words in that book, like the very fitting logophilia[20].

After dinner, I helped Viola clear and do the dishes (it was our turn, which was cool since it was such an easy night because of the takeout), walked Bob and fed him his dinner, then headed upstairs to do my homework. I knocked on the door of my old room, since I had to get some stuff from my desk. I figured I would work in the study; I had some research to do on the computer anyway. But when I went in, Juliet was all nice and chatty again. "Do your homework in here," she said. "It's okay. You won't bother me."

[20]logophilia: fondness for or love of words

So I stayed for a while. We didn't talk much, since we both had a lot to do. Then I had to hit the computer, so I packed up my things and headed for the study. I wanted to check my e-mail, too. I was hoping Poppy might have something to say about the final clue.

Helena was coming out of the study as I was going in. In fact, we nearly ran into each other. "Whoa!" she said, hiding something behind her back.

"What's that?" I asked, trying to reach around her to see.

"Nothing. Math homework. I mean, a paper for language arts. Nothing." Helena held the paper away from me, turned, and ran into her and Viola's room, slamming the door behind her.

That was weird. And a little suspicious. Were Helena and Viola getting somewhere with that list of numbers? No way did I want them to beat us again, especially not on this clue, the one that really counted. I went over and tapped on their door.

"Go away!" said Helena.

"I just wanted to see —"

"Forget it!" Helena again. I heard her and Viola giggling.

This could mean trouble.

Chapter Twenty

I gave up on Helena and Viola, turned around, and went into the study. It was a waste of time to try to get anything out of them. Helena's behavior made me nervous, though. Exactly how close *were* they to solving the final clue?

The computer was already on, so I signed on quickly. There was a short message from Poppy. The bad news? He didn't offer any ideas about the clue. The good news? He said he'd probably be home by Saturday!

Next, I clicked on a message from Emma. It was addressed to both me and Zoe, and the subject line was "NEWSFLASH," but that could mean anything. She forwards a lot of silly stuff that I usually just delete, but I always check first to make sure it's nothing important.

This was important.

To: WrrdGrrl; Zoeth
From: EMMA64
Subject: NEWSFLASH
Just finished dinner, and it's too late to call, so I hope, hope, hope you get this. Dance class was canceled, so I spent

141

some more time thinking about the clue. I had an IDEA!!! I decided that maybe the numbers each meant something about the treasure and its location. Like, what if the treasure is in a box, 24 inches by one foot in size??? And what if it's buried somewhere? So I did an experiment. I paced off the distance from the other places where we've found the answers to clues. And guess what I found out? You'll never guess, so I'll tell you!!! If you pace off 974 paces from Mrs. Sparrow's house, and 317 paces from the McDaniel Residence, you come to a spot on the green that is exactly 112 paces from the Nguyens' store!!! Is that wild, or what? (I figure the 113 in the clue is to the OTHER side of the one-foot box.)

I took two sticks and put them in a cross at the place where everything came together, near the gazebo.

Anyway, maybe you think this is nuts. And I can't figure out any of the other numbers. But let's talk some more at lunch tomorrow. Maybe this is it! Maybe we're about to be rich! Rich! RICH! RICH! beyond our wildest dreams!!!!! :-)

E.

Wow. I read Emma's message once, then read it again, getting more and more excited. This was by far the best idea she'd come up with yet! Emma was on to something. I just knew it. I read it one more time, printed it out, then signed off, since there was no other mail for me.

I had to see the clue again. I ran to my room for

the crumpled receipt I'd been carrying around. Then I headed for Juliet's room.

"Check this out," I said, giving her the printout of Emma's message. I sat down on her inflatable chair to study the clue again. I stared at the numbers for the millionth time:

24/1
1999
14:50
974.317
112–113

By the time she had finished reading, I'd figured out another number. "What if the box was buried in 1999?" I said, before she could even comment on Emma's idea. "I bet that's it!"

Juliet came over to look at the clue with me. "Definitely," she said. "This is great! I just *know* Emma has to be right."

"So we only have one more number to get," I said. "What could this mean?" I tapped on the numbers 14:50. I looked around the room, hoping for inspiration. Then my eye fell on Juliet's digital clock. The numbers read 10:32. "That's it!" I cried, jumping up so fast that the chair fell over. "It's a time!"

"Uh, Ophelia?" Juliet asked. "The clock only goes up to twelve."

I shook my head. "Not in military time. Or police time. Didn't you ever hear Miranda or Mom use police time? It's a twenty-four hour system, with twelve meaning noon. So 14:50 would be . . ." I figured it out, "two-fifty P.M." I was pacing around the room, too excited to stay still. "I bet — I bet that's when we're supposed to dig up the box! Two-fifty, right after school!"

Juliet stared at me. "Ophelia, we got it," she whispered. "We got it," she repeated, a little louder. "We won!" she almost shouted.

"Shhh!" I said. "Don't let the twins hear."

Juliet had jumped onto her bed and now she was bouncing up and down. "We'll be rich!" she shout-whispered gleefully. "The fortune is ours! By tomorrow, our lives will be changed!"

"Unless somebody else digs first," I said, thinking that some other team might have also figured out the clue.

Juliet nodded slowly. "You're right. You're absolutely right. We have to sneak out there and dig tonight."

"Us? Dig?" As soon as she said it, I knew she was right. We had to get out there before anybody else. "Right," I said. "What time should we go out?"

"We'll have to wait until Mom's asleep," said Juliet. "How about — midnight?"

Suddenly, I horripilated[21]. This was getting exciting. "Yeah," I said. "Midnight."

"We'll need light," said Juliet.

"And shovels. I'll round up some stuff and put it right outside the back door where we can get it without making noise."

Juliet glanced at the clock. "What about Katherine?" she asked.

We looked at each other for a second. "Why not?" I asked finally. "We did say she could be on the team. But I don't see how we can get Emma and Zoe in on it. It's way too late to call them."

"They'll forgive us when they get their share of the prize," said Juliet. She reached over and turned off her light.

"Girls?" Mom called from downstairs. "Almost ready for bed?"

I opened the door. "Just going," I called back down. I winked at Juliet and tapped on my watch. "Midnight," I mouthed. "We'll meet at the back door."

She nodded. "I'll tell Katherine," she whispered. She started tiptoeing down the hall toward Katherine's room.

After a quick e-mail update to Poppy (I didn't mention our midnight expedition) I went into my

[21]horripilated: got goose bumps

room and waited until I heard Mom go upstairs and into the study. Then I slipped into the upstairs part of the barn. I rummaged through our camping stuff until I found a flashlight that worked. Then, lighting my way with it, I tiptoed down the barn stairs and over to Poppy's gardening corner, where he keeps all his flowerpots, fertilizers, and tools. There were two shovels on the rack. I also found an oversized trowel he uses for planting tulip bulbs. That might come in handy. And I grabbed a couple of the torches we use to light the garden for parties on summer nights. It took me a couple of trips, but I brought everything out to the back door. Luckily, the mudroom[22] is just inside that door, which meant it would be easy to grab our boots and jackets.

I took a flashlight back into the barn and upstairs. Before I opened the door back into the house, I stood with my ear to it, listening to make sure nobody was moving around in the hall. Then, quickly, I opened it and slipped in. I took three quick steps and opened the door to my own room.

There was a note on my pillow. *K's in*, it said. Juliet's writing. *C U @ 12.*

---

[22]mudroom: a room added on outside a main door, where muddy outdoor things can be left in order to keep the house cleaner. Ours is usually packed with boots, shoes, skis, bike helmets, soccer gear, dog toys, and whatever else we toss in there.

I sat down on my bed and set my alarm. Not that I'd need it. There was no way I was going to fall asleep between now and midnight. I was too excited.

Instead of changing into the T-shirt I usually sleep in, I just took off my jeans and got under the covers. I read for a while, but I was having trouble concentrating on the words. My mind kept slipping back to the treasure. Finally, I turned off the light and just lay there, thinking. What was going to be in that box? Money? Gold and jewels? I fantasized about what kind of treasures a man like Grandpa Grover might have collected. He'd been president of a company that made airplane parts, so maybe he'd traveled all over the world. There might be treasures from faraway places, like ancient jade from China, or gold from Peru. I pictured a pile of diamonds, straight from a mine. Maybe there'd be crown jewels from the kings and queens of Europe!

I saw myself reaching into a brass-bound wooden treasure chest, coming up with a dripping handful of emeralds and rubies. "I'm rich!" I cried.

Then the alarm went off.

I groaned and rolled over to check my clock. 11:52. It was time to get up.

Chapter Twenty-one

I got into my jeans and pulled on a sweater. Then I cracked my door open to peek out into the hall. I didn't see any light or hear anyone moving around, so I opened the door the rest of the way and stepped out, hoping Bob was fast asleep on his bed in my parents' room. All I needed was for him to start barking.

Just then, Katherine came tiptoeing down the hall, with Juliet behind her. We grinned at one another, but didn't say a word.

The three of us padded noiselessly to the door to the barn. Then we found our way to the barn stairs, let ourselves outside, and slipped around to the back door. The cold seeped through my slippers, and the air was chilly. I was glad to pull on boots and a jacket from inside the mudroom.

We grabbed the shovels and torches. "Ready?" I whispered.

"Ready," whispered Katherine and Juliet.

We walked across the street and toward the green, staying out of the circle of light cast by the streetlight. There was no moon out, but the stars were bright and clear. Everything was very, very quiet. My breath fogged in front of me as I walked along with the shovel over my shoulder. We didn't need to light the torches, since there was enough light from the streetlight to find our way to the old gazebo. In a few moments we stood next to it. The gazebo loomed crookedly in the shadows, looking creepy with its peeling paint and leaning pillars.

From there, we looked across the green to the old school. There was a light on in the lobby area of the McDaniel Residence, but I figured all the residents must be asleep. That light must stay on all night. Other than that, the only visible lights were streetlights and the blue glow of a television from a few upstairs rooms, where people must be watching late-night TV.

"If we walk straight toward the old school from here, we'll probably find the X Emma left," Juliet whispered. She shifted her shovel to the other shoulder.

Katherine and I nodded. I looked at the old building and walked toward it. Beyond the gazebo was that tangle of weeds where the old fountain used to be. I checked in the other direction to see if I was also in a straight line with the Nguyens' store. A clump of trees was sort of in the way, but I was sure we were in the right area.

"It has to be around here somewhere," hissed Katherine, "but I can't see a thing. I'm going to get some light here."

"No!" I hissed back, but it was too late. She'd already lit her torch. Oh, well. She was right. We'd never find the X without a little light.

"There it is!" I said, louder than I'd meant to, when the flickering light hit two sticks on the ground, crossed to make an unmistakable X. My heart was beating hard.

"Stay there! Don't move!" whispered Juliet. "We'll bring the shovels over."

In two seconds, Katherine and Juliet were there with the shovels and trowel. I set up the torches for light while they started to dig.

"The ground is soft," Juliet whispered. "Like somebody dug here recently. I thought the chest was buried in 1999."

"Maybe Mr. Drudge just checked on it," I whispered back.

"Speaking of Mr. Drudge," whispered Katherine, "do you think it's going to count if we dig this up at the wrong time?" She had stopped shoveling for a second.

Juliet and I stared at her. I had never even thought of that. But it was too late to change our plans now. I *had* to find that treasure chest first! "Just dig," I said.

We dug for what seemed like a long time, but it was probably only a few minutes, since the hole wasn't all that deep when Juliet's shovel hit something that made a loud "clunk."

We all gasped. "That must be it!" I said. I grabbed the trowel and bent into the hole to scrape the dirt aside.

I strained my eyes to see into the dimly lit hole. "Can you tilt one of the torches this way?" I asked Katherine. "I can't see."

She grabbed a torch and held it so that it cast much more light into the hole. I caught a sudden sparkle, as if there was something metallic down there. I grabbed the trowel again and dug some more, frantically.

"More light!" I said. "More light!"

Then I saw it.

It wasn't a brass-bound wooden box.

It wasn't even a metal tool box.

It wasn't a box at all.

"It's a pipe," I said. "Plumbing. We found plumbing."

Chapter Twenty-two

"Plumbing?" Juliet demanded.

I got up off my knees and dusted off my hands, which were freezing from the cold dirt. "Plumbing," I said. I sighed. "Probably for the fountain."

Katherine let out an exasperated sigh. "*Now* what?" she asked.

"We dig again," Juliet said. "It has to be around here somewhere." She grabbed a shovel.

"I don't think so," said a voice from the darkness.

And Miranda stepped forward, into the light of our torches.

"Miranda!" I gasped. "What are you doing here?"

"What do you think?" she asked, gesturing at her uniform. "I'm on duty, and this is an official visit." She shook her head at us. "Torches?" she asked. "Very dramatic, but not exactly secretive. Next time you dig for buried treasure you might want to use something a little less — showy."

"Did somebody see us?" I asked.

Miranda nodded. "Oh, yes," she said. "We had a

call from a concerned citizen. A Mr. Edwin Drudge."

I gasped again. "Mr. Drudge called the police?"

Miranda smiled. "Not only that, but he gave us a message to pass along to you," she said. She pulled out her detective-in-training notebook and flipped it open, holding it near one of the torches so she could read from it. "He said to tell you to go home to bed," she reported. "He said to tell you that you're not even close. He said to tell you that the fortune won't be found underground."

"But how — ?" asked Juliet. "Never mind."

I knew what she was thinking. Mr. Drudge seemed to be everywhere.

Miranda made us put out the torches. Then she marched the three of us back home. "I won't tell Mom, as long as you promise never to do something so silly ever again," she told us.

Chapter Twenty-three

We promised. What else could we do? Then we said good-bye to Miranda and snuck back inside.

I pulled off my jeans, changed into my sleep shirt, and fell into bed. The next thing I knew, Juliet was waking me up. "Ophelia," she said, lifting the pillow off my head. "Wake up!"

"What is it?" I asked, rolling over to look at my clock. It was three in the morning! "No more digging," I groaned. "Please."

She sat down on my bed. "It's not that," she said. "I had a bad dream. A really bad one. About this monster that lived in the barn. It was all dark and hairy and —" She shuddered. "Ophelia, will you come sleep in our room?"

Our room. I hadn't heard her say that in a long time.

I woke up the next morning to the sound of Juliet whispering in my ear. She was sitting next to me on the bed, holding a pillow away from my head. "Time to get up," she said softly. "Wake up, sleepyhead."

I rubbed my eyes. For a second it felt as if everything was back to normal. Then I remembered. I was sleeping in Juliet's bed. She'd let me have it, while she slept on her chair. I yawned and gazed out the window. It was nice to wake up in that room again.

"Ophelia?" Juliet asked.

"Hmm?" I wasn't quite awake yet.

"Do you like your new room?" She mushed the pillow she was holding, not looking at me.

"Sure, I guess. It's okay. Why?"

"I was just thinking," she answered. "Would you — would you consider moving back in here?"

"What?" *Now* I was awake. I sat up. "You mean it? You want to share a room again?"

She nodded. "I think so."

"You *think* so?" That wasn't enough. "What if I move back in and you change your mind? I'm not going through that again."

"I won't. Change my mind, I mean." She mushed the pillow some more. "At least, not for a long time. I guess I'm just not really ready to live alone after all." Juliet met my eyes. "I miss you. It's boring in here without you."

"I miss you, too," I said. "Even your snoring. And I miss our windows."

We worked it all out. We decided to keep the junk room as an extra space we could use. I'd move my bed back into our room, but we'd put one of our chairs in there, and one of our desks. That way, if one of us wanted to do our homework or just hang out alone, she could be in the little room. If we wanted to be together, we could do that, too. It was the perfect solution.

We were roommates again, as well as teammates. All we had to do now was solve the final clue — for real, this time — and life would be perfect.

Chapter Twenty-four

"*Ferdinand*! How about *Ferdinand*?" I hugged the book to my chest. "I always loved this one. Remember? It's about the bull who's supposed to do bullfights, but he just wants to sniff flowers?"

It was the next afternoon, after school. Juliet and I were in our room (we'd already moved my bed back in and rearranged things), looking through our old books. Our team hadn't gotten any further with the clue, though Emma was working hard on figuring out if the numbers had any relation to one another. She thought there might be some kind of pattern in their sequence, and she was trying all kinds of calculations to figure out what it might be. Meanwhile, we'd all realized that we were supposed to go to the library that very afternoon, bringing a favorite book to donate.

I plopped down on the floor to page through *Ferdinand.* Could I really give this one away? It meant a lot to me. Mom and Poppy used to read aloud to us every night when we were little, and for a while I picked *Ferdinand* every single time it was my turn to choose.

"What about this one?" asked Juliet, holding up

an old, tattered copy of *The Runaway Bunny.* "I always loved the pictures. They're so — I don't know — cozy."

"I love that book, too," I said. "But maybe you should find one that's in better shape." I put *Ferdinand* aside for the moment and poked through some of the other books on the lower shelf of my bookcase, where I keep old favorites. Just seeing their covers brought back so many good memories. Madeleine, in her broad-brimmed hat. Doctor De Soto, the friendly dentist. The oh-so-colorful Very Hungry Caterpillar. They were like a bunch of old friends to me.

"This is it!" cried Juliet, pulling out a book. *"Where the Wild Things Are.* This has to be my all-time favorite. Don't you love the costume Max wears when he goes off to meet the Wild Things in the jungle?" She flipped through the book. "I used to think the Wild Things were so scary. But Max gets to be their king because he looks them in the eye. I always thought that was the coolest." She read right through to the last page. "And then Max comes back home to find his supper waiting, 'still hot.' It's like, you can go off and have all these adventures, but home is always there for you, too." She closed the book. "I'm bringing this one," she said, looking at it fondly. "Some other kid will love it as much as I did."

"And I guess I'll bring *Ferdinand*," I said. "Mr. Drudge did say we should bring a favorite. And anyway, it'll always be there if I want it."

I pulled a book off the top shelf of my bookcase. "Might as well return this while I'm there," I said. It was a library book, *Summer of My German Soldier*. I'd finished it a couple of days before. I opened the back cover to make sure it wasn't overdue.

Juliet was vacillating[23]. "Or maybe I should bring *Curious George*," she said, pulling out another book. "I always thought that monkey was so funny, always getting into trouble."

"Juliet," I said. I was staring down at the card pocket in the back of my library book. "Do you know the library's exact address?"

"What?" she asked. "Why would I? I never send them mail."

"I don't, either," I said. "That's why I never knew that their address is Twenty-four First Street. That's what it says, right here underneath their name." The library's name and address were stamped on the card pocket.

"Huh," Juliet said. "Interesting. I mean, *Not*."

"You're wrong," I said. "It's *very* interesting. Especially when you notice that it also says something else under the name."

[23]vacillating: being indecisive

Juliet put down Curious George and came over to see. I pointed to the stamp. "Walker Memorial Library," we read out loud at the same time. "Established 1999. Twenty-four First Street."

Juliet grabbed my shoulder. "Those are the first two numbers in the clue," she said. She ran back to her bed and rummaged around in her backpack, coming up with the rumpled receipt she'd been given at the store. Together, we looked at the list of numbers. Suddenly, it all began to make sense.

"That must be a Dewey Decimal number," Juliet said, pointing to the fourth one on the list. "So the clue is talking about a book!"

"And that last set must be page numbers!" I said. "But what does the one in between mean? Fourteen fifty." I started to pace, thinking hard. "Fourteen fifty. How does fourteen relate to fifty?"

"I'm getting Katherine," said Juliet. She ran out of the room. I kept pacing, waiting for them to come back.

"I've got it!" I said, the second they came into the room. "Vermont! Something about Vermont. We were the fourteenth state to join the union. Fourteen of fifty, get it? Maybe the book is in the Vermont section!"

"Got it," Katherine said, nodding. "Let's go."

"Where?" Juliet asked.

"To the library," Katherine said.

There was no time to waste. If we'd figured it out, somebody else probably had, too. These numbers were going to lead to a book. And I wanted us to be the first ones to find it.

We grabbed the books we were planning to donate. I called Emma and Zoe and told them where to meet us. Then we flew out of the house. We ran practically the whole way to the library, cutting through the church's backyard and going through the field in back, running over the footbridge that crosses the stream and charging up the hill. I glanced back once and saw that Helena and Viola were behind us, and catching up quickly. They must have seen us run out of the house.

We ran past the elementary school, hung a right at the corner of First Street, and came panting up to the library's front walk. I looked at the building. The street number was right there, in big brass numbers over the door. And, now that I looked, I noticed the carved granite cornerstone that read 1999. How could we have been so dense?

Helena and Viola caught up just as we pulled open the big glass doors. A bunch of other kids were coming up the walk at the same time, books under their arms. Of course! It was the designated time for us all to come.

"This way." I gestured as we entered the library. I headed toward the back corner of the reading room. It's a tucked-away little spot, hidden behind the nonfiction shelves. All the Vermont books are kept there, and there's a little table with a lamp where you can sit to do research.

Mr. Drudge was sitting at the table, reading a book. He looked up when we approached and smiled his thin little smile. "Well, well," he said. "The Parker girls. Welcome."

I turned to see that Helena and Viola were right behind us. So were a bunch of kids from other teams. They must have figured out that we knew something, by the way we ran into the library.

I nodded to Mr. Drudge, but there was no time for polite chitchat. I turned to the shelves and started tracing my finger along the bottom of each shelved book, trying to find the book numbered 974.317. "Nine seventy-one, nine seventy-three," I said out loud. "Nine seventy-four!" Then I went down a shelf and kept looking. It wasn't on that shelf, either, since that row ended at 974.313. I got down on my knees. "Hey!" I said. I poked my finger into an empty slot. "It's supposed to be right here."

Juliet, Emma, Zoe, and Katherine were right with me. "Wait," said Juliet. "You mean, somebody took it out?"

"The one book we're looking for?" asked Zoe. "Unbelievable!"

Just then, Mr. Drudge cleared his throat. We all looked over at him, and he closed the book he was reading with a snap.

I stared at him. He looked back at me.

He smiled.

"That's it, isn't it?" I asked. "That's the book we're supposed to find."

"Congratulations," he said, handing it over.

Chapter Twenty-five

I took the book. My hands were shaking a little. I read the title out loud. *"History of Cloverdale, Vermont."*

"Turn to page one-twelve!" Juliet urged.

I looked around. There were tons of kids there by then. Probably every team in the treasure hunt was standing around, staring at me. That's when I realized that Mr. Drudge — and Grandpa Grover — must have planned it this way. They wanted everybody there when the final treasure was found.

I opened the book and turned to page one hundred twelve. There, between page one-twelve and page one-thirteen, was an envelope. I picked it up and saw that page one-thirteen was a full-page black-and-white picture. A picture of a very familiar place, easy to recognize even though it looked very different. It was the green. Except, the gazebo looked brand-new. There was a brass band sitting inside it, playing for the people gathered around. And the fountain stood nearby, water sparkling in the sun. Little kids played in the basin, while their mothers sat nearby, watching. A group of people were playing softball in another corner of the green, and picnickers were gathered in little clumps under trees. "Wow," I said. "That's so cool." I just stared at the picture for a moment, thinking how great it would be if the green looked like that again.

"What are you *doing*?" asked Juliet. "Open the envelope!"

I handed her the book so she and the others could see the picture. The book was passed from hand to hand as I tore open the envelope and pulled out two pieces of paper. One was a check for fifty thousand dollars. The space where it read, "Pay to the Order of" was blank. I looked at the long string of zeros and felt my stomach flip over. That was a *lot* of money. Maybe it wasn't James Grover's *entire* fortune, but it was a fortune to me! And my team had won it! "We won!" I said, holding up the check so everyone could see. "We did it!"

Everybody started talking at once. Then Mr. Drudge cleared his throat again, which was enough to quiet us down.

"Read the letter," he suggested.

I looked at the other piece of paper I was holding. "Out loud?" I asked, looking back at Mr. Drudge.

He nodded.

I looked at the bottom of the letter. "It's from Grandpa Grover," I said. I took a deep breath. "'Dear Treasure Hunters,'" I read. "'I hope you've enjoyed yourselves. As you solved each mystery along the way, you've also begun to learn about your town and the people in it. If everything went according to my plan, this treasure hunt will change Cloverdale forever. Change usually means progress, but in this case, change means going backward. Back to a time when Cloverdale was a place where an old woman would never be in need of help or company. When children knew and respected their town's history. When a fountain was a gathering place. When newcomers were made welcome, and when you could get anything you needed without getting into a car. And when knowledge and learning were highly valued and started at the youngest ages. Cloverdale will be a community again, with places where people meet to shop and talk and spend time together. Cloverdale will once more be the kind of town it was when I was a boy.

"'Now, there's one last mystery for you to solve. I want you to guess what I, Grandpa Grover, would have most wanted you, the treasure hunters, to do with the fortune you've found.'"

Chapter Twenty-six

The last mystery was the easiest. That day, all the teams got together in the children's room, first to hand over their books and then to talk and make plans.

We worked hard for the rest of the week to pull it together, but by Saturday night our work paid off. That evening, the entire town gathered for an old-fashioned potluck dinner in the old auditorium. Kids and their parents had worked together to set up tables and chairs, and spread them with red paper tablecloths donated by the Nguyens. The red curtains were cleaned and hanging straight, and the room was decorated with red and white balloons we'd spent hours blowing up.

Two whole tables were covered with pots and bowls and platters of food, and people talked happily as they helped themselves. When everybody was settled, my teammates and I (yes, including Katherine) walked up the stairs to the stage, to stand beside an easel that held a big piece of poster board, covered by a sheet.

The crowd didn't quiet down until Zoe gave one

of her trademark piercing whistles. Then, suddenly, the room was dead quiet.

"We have an announcement to make," I said. My team had nominated me to do the talking. I was flattered at the time, but now I was nervous. I glanced down at the nearest table, where Viola, Helena, and Miranda were sitting with Mom — and with Poppy, who'd made it home just in time. I smiled at him, and he winked at me. Olivia was crouched by the stage, shooting pictures. I spotted Mrs. Sparrow, sitting with some of the McDaniel residents we'd gotten to know. I smiled at them, too, and at the Nguyen family, who were at the next table over. Then I started to talk. "We are the official winners of the treasure hunt, since we were the first to solve the final clue," I said, checking the notes I'd brought onstage. "But one thing we figured out is that it didn't really matter who was first. In the long run, the real treasure was learning about our town, and learning to work together to make things better here. So, in that spirit, we worked together to figure out what Grandpa — I mean, Mr. Grover — would have wanted us to do with this prize." I held up the check. Everybody knew what it was, since Olivia and Janie had done another story for the paper, featuring a picture of me and my teammates holding up the check and grinning like idiots.

"We've decided he would have wanted this fortune to bring good fortune to the whole town, so we're donating this money to fix up the gazebo and the fountain and the green so that next summer we can all enjoy days like this," I said, pulling aside the sheet to display a huge blown-up copy of the picture from page 113.

The crowd burst into applause. My teammates and I had a big group hug, right up there on the stage. (Katherine took the opportunity to whisper, "Couldn't you just have kept a couple hundred? Think of all the shopping we could have done.") As I squeezed their shoulders, I looked over into the wings where Mr. Drudge was standing. He gave me a nod and a smile. Not his usual thin smile, either.

This time, he was absolutely beaming.

About the Author

Ellen Miles lives in a small house in Vermont with her large dog, Django, who can eat a maple cree-mee in the time it takes to say "maple creemee." She has one brother and one sister, both older, and while she loves her siblings, she always thought it might be fun to have many more of them. One of her all-time favorite books is *Harriet the Spy*. She loves to ride her bike in the summer and ski in the winter, so Vermont is the perfect place for her to live.